Mysteries You Can't Put Down

Stories of Intrigue By Brad Bennett.

CONTENTS

THE SECRET OF THE UNDEAD ROOM

"911 Emergency; how may I help you?"

"I want to report a murder!"

"Where are you?"

"The Sylvia Hotel, room 802." The woman's voice was trembling.

"Okay, stay calm, ma'am. Who has been murdered?"

"My boss, R.K. Fielding. I just found him dead. I'm his secretary, Mary Barton."

"Are you sure he's dead?"

"Yes, he's been killed. There's a knife in his head. It's awful."

"Okay. Listen carefully, Mary, leave the room, touch nothing. The Police will be there shortly."

A strange, buzzing, nattering insect kept attacking Ed. He batted at it, swatted at it, but it wouldn't go away. He leaped up in his bed in a final desperate attempt to kill it.

Then he awoke!

Damn! It was that god-awful alarm tone he had set. Ed grappled for his phone, mad at himself for selecting that app. He hit the cell's answer button.

"Yeah," he muttered.

"It's central dispatch. We've got a homicide over at The Sylvia Hotel near Stanley Park. You better get down there right away."

Ed glanced at the time—1:00 a.m. "C'mon, you guys! I just came off a long surveillance operation. Bill can cover it; he's my teams best guy."

"Sorry, Ed, it's Sunday morning. We're short-handed, and the Chief wants you on this anyway. It's turning into a possible media shit-bag, big names involved."

"Alright, alright, I'm on it!"

Ed was waiting out on the street below his bachelor apartment when the squad car drove up. He flashed his police ID card to the driver. He didn't need to; every cop on the force would recognize Chief Inspector Edwin Steelside. At fifty-seven, he was the most senior-ranking detective in Homicide. Ed settled his tall, angular frame into the front seat. The car pulled out into the quiet late-hour street and sped off towards Stanley Park, a vast natural area that skirts the city's northern beaches.

"You hear what's going on?" Ed asked the young officer driving.

"Not much; something's up at The Sylvia Hotel. That damn place has been giving us disturbance calls all night. There's a big media event going on over there, some kind of zombie festival; lots of loonies on the loose."

Ed winced. "Zombies? God, that's all I need."

As they neared the park's southern side bordering on English Bay, Ed reflected on his memories of The Sylvia Hotel. It was an old Vancouver landmark, a throwback to the brick and mortar buildings that once made up the city in the early 1900's. It had been recently refurbished, with a new modern high-rise tower added on the property. But the old section remained, and it reflected the glamour and class of an earlier age. It was now a popular site for events and a prominent location for the nostalgia crowd; the vine-covered structure evoked the atmosphere of the old movies.

At the rear of the hotel, Deputy Inspector Bill Doland was waiting for Ed's arrival. Bill was new on the force, but this younger, athletic man's savvy for grasping street life had impressed Ed, and he soon rose in status on Ed's team. The two men met, then entered through a side door.

"We're up on the top floor," Bill informed Ed over the clamor of the packed crowd. "Looks bad! Some big Hollywood poobah's been murdered. We've sealed the area and kept the scene isolated."

"Good," Ed nodded. "Sorry, I'm a bit late."

They pushed through a chaos of pretending, stumbling zombies all decked out in undead costumes. A rock band was pounding out loud hallucinogenic music. Various zombies wandered awkwardly around the dance floor, miming what only they could imagine how the walking dead might dance.

As they neared the elevator, a swaying zombie wobbled in front of Ed, blocking his way. Ed tried to brush past the guy, but the zombie wouldn't move. Instead, the guy opened up his shirt, revealing a chest covered in fake blood; phony entrails fell from his belly. He snarled like a rabid animal.

"Get away from me, you God damn freak!" Ed yelled in his face. "You like gore, huh?" Ed grabbed him by the shirt. "How 'bout I show you a real mutilated body? Let's see if you can handle that?"

The zombie reeled back in fear. Bill came forward and put his hand on Eds arm. "Easy, Ed!" He shouted over the confusion. "We're all on edge here, and there's a lot of press guys around!"

Ed pushed the stunned zombie away, and they got on the elevator.

When they arrived on the 8th floor, a stocky security man was standing by. He began briefing the two detectives as they walked down the hallway towards room 802.

"I'm Bruce Allmon, Head of Security," he told them. "I was on scene about five minutes after we received the call from 911.

I found the woman who called it in standing outside the door. No people, other than her, and I, have been in that room."

"Why did you go into the room?" Ed frowned.

"I had to. I have to inspect any incident in this hotel for safety and security reasons. I touched nothing. I came out and stood here outside the room guarding this floor."

"Alright then, I'll let you open the door, but please remain outside."

The hotel room had the rich scent of polished mahogany, and the fixtures were of gleaming brass. It was one of the largest rooms, a suite with a bar and other amenities.

Ed's eyes went to the body lying face up in the middle of the floor. Protruding grotesquely from the victim's forehead was a sizable wooden-handled knife. It had penetrated into the man's skull. There were small specks of blood spattered around on the carpet. The deceased was dressed in evening clothes and there appeared to be no signs of a struggle.

Ed kneeled close to the body. The victim was positioned almost as if he were sleeping. That seemed odd, Ed thought. The violent blow the man had suffered undoubtedly would have left him lying more askew. The hit appeared to have been so powerful that it had pushed back part of his skull, laying bare some of the brain's dura matter.

"Whoever did this really had it in for this guy," Ed observed.

"For sure," Bill replied. "If you've ever watched a zombie movie, this is exactly how they kill the walking dead—a stab in the brain."

"What is this then, some kinda movie-style message?"

Before Bill could answer, a knock came on the door. Bill opened it, and Bruce informed them the crime scene photographer had arrived. Ed rose from his examination of the body.

"All right," he concluded, "I've seen enough here. Let's look at the rest of this apartment."

He motioned to the photographer. "Follow me." They began walking towards the bedroom.

"I want every inch of this apartment videoed," he told the man. "Door locks, window locks, everything."

Then he motioned to Bill. "Okay, let's talk to the woman who found the body."

An older, well-dressed matronly woman was waiting in a sitting area across from the elevators. She was visibly upset. Her face was stained and streaked from the tears that had run down her makeup. She didn't even look up when Ed sat down next to her.

"Mrs. Barton," Ed greeted her, "I'm police detective Ed Steelside. They have assigned me to this crime. I'm going to ask you some questions. Just recollect the events of tonight the best that you can."

Ed clicked on his cell to record the conversation. "What is your relationship with the deceased?"

Mary wiped her eyes. She spoke as best she could, even though her throat was raw from all her crying. "He is—was my boss, Roland K. Fielding. He's the President and CEO of The UnDead Movie Studios."

"And your position there?"

"I was his personal secretary. I took care of his appointments, helped in his script and film production."

"Is your room on this floor?"

"Yes, all the UnDead staff have rooms reserved on this floor."

"Mary, how were you able to walk right into his room?"

The woman took out a medicine capsule she still had in her purse. "It was 1:00 a.m. I was bringing this to RK. It's his meds—he'd run out and I had the backup. RK knew I was coming, so he left his room unlocked. I knocked and went in."

"He called you at that time, 1:00 a.m?"

"No, no. RK reminded me earlier at the party table downstairs. He told me to bring him his medicine around that time. He mentioned he would be in a meeting in his room, and didn't want to be disturbed until then."

"What time was that downstairs?"

"10 p.m. roughly; I'm not sure."

"You remained downstairs until when?"

"I came up here sometime after midnight, maybe 12:30."

Ed shifted in his chair. He adjusted his cell and continued, "Did anyone leave with your boss when he left the table downstairs?"

"Yes, Arvin Blackstone, our studio's executive producer. I overheard RK tell Arvin they should go upstairs to the privacy of his room."

"Did your boss give you any sign of why he wanted this private meeting?"

"No, but it must have been important." Mary had to reflect for a moment. "It was noisy, and everyone was drinking, so maybe he thought that was more appropriate."

Ed leaned in closer to emphasize his words. "Do you remember Arvin's demeanor when he left that table? Did he appear happy, sad, upset? What was his emotional state?"

"Oh, he seemed happy; everyone was in a good mood. The festival was a promo hit, and our new movie's previews were going well."

"Who remained at the table with you?"

"Um, oh, I think Cal Morrow, the shows chief writer and associate producer."

"Alright, Mary, and when did Cal leave the table?"

"About an hour later, I think. Cal complained he wasn't feeling well, woozy or something. I'm not sure. It had been a long day. We were all drinking a bit."

It was clear to Ed that Mary was tiring. "That's enough for now, Mary, but I want you to please keep this quiet, not talk to anyone else about this. Do you understand?"

"Yes, I understand."

Ed snapped off his cell.

Bill Doland was by the elevator reviewing a list of UnDead Studio employees attending the festival when Ed walked over.

"Bill, I've noticed there are hotel security cameras everywhere. What have you found out about them?"

"All eight floors of the hotel are fully surveyed. The hotel's manager, Darin Lawson, told me the hotel has all the latest tech, so we're good there."

"Great, when can he turn the videos over?"

"That's a problem. The guy won't answer until he checks with his lawyers. He's playing hardball with us."

"Good God, Bill! This is a homicide investigation."

"I've run across this before with hotels, Ed. They're squeamish as hell about filming guests. They want to check for any embarrassing stuff."

"All right, we can wait, but keep after him. We need those videos as soon as possible. I need to talk to that security guy now."

Bruce Allmon was busy talking on his cell. He clicked it off as Ed approached.

"Okay, Bruce, just a few questions. Don't worry about this recording. It's routine." Ed turned on his cell.

"What was your first impression when you entered room 802?"

"My first instinct was to go forward and check the body. But it was quite obvious the guy was a goner; there was a big freaking knife stuck in his head."

"Did you step into any of the blood spatter near the body?"

"God, no!" Bruce flinched, shaking his head. "I skirted

around it and walked to the bedroom. I wanted to check and make sure the place was empty."

"So, after checking everything, did you then leave?"

"For sure, my only thought then was to secure this entire floor."

Ed snapped off his cell. "Thanks, Bruce. I want to remind you not to discuss this incident with anyone for now."

Bill was still going over the occupant's list for the seventh floor when Ed walked back over.

"I've notified everyone I can," Bill informed him. "But I still can't find Blackstone. He isn't in his room, and this other guy, Cal Morrow, hasn't answered his door."

"Okay, let's try it again. If he still doesn't answer, we'll use the passkey."

The two men went down the hall to the room noted, and Ed rapped on the door. "Mr. Morrow!" Ed yelled. "This is the Police! Please open your door!"

When it looked like he wasn't coming Ed pulled out the passkey, but before he could use it, the door opened!

"Yes!" A man of about forty answered. He was disheveled, as if he had been sleeping with his clothes on.

"Are you Cal Morrow?" Ed asked.

"Yes, what's going on?"

"Why didn't you open your door? We've knocked on it on several occasions."

"I, I haven't been feeling well," Cal stammered. "I didn't know you guys were out here. What's going on? Why are you banging on my door?"

"Have you been drinking?"

"I had a few drinks, but I'm not a heavy drinker. We all were having a good time."

"When you were at the party earlier, what time did you leave and come up to your room?"

"Um, I don't know. I didn't check the time."

Ed made his tone more forceful. "Did you meet with anyone up here when you left that party downstairs?"

"No. I'm sure I didn't. I told you I was feeling drowsy!"

"You didn't meet with R.K. Fielding, your boss, go to his room?"

"No, no. Look, I told you. What do you want from me?" Cal was now becoming agitated. Ed decided he wouldn't go any further.

"Mr. Morrow," Ed told him, "I'm sorry to inform you that your boss, Roland K. Fielding, was found dead in his room just over an hour ago."

"Oh, my God!" Cal reeled backward, staggering. He leaned against the door for support.

"You cannot go back to your room now," Ed added. "We'll ask the hotel to put you up somewhere else for tonight. Also, you must remain in the Vancouver area. We will talk to you again. Do you understand?"

"Yes, I understand," Cal groaned. "Can I at least go back and get my overnight case?"

"Okay, but we will have to check it as you leave. Also, I want to remind you to please stay available. We'll want to talk to you again."

Bill was still completing his list of the employees and he wasn't happy. He motioned over to Ed. "I still haven't found Blackstone; he's not in his room. This guy has to be somewhere else in the hotel or he's left the building."

"How about all the other UnDead employees?"

"They're all accounted for; the only people on this floor during the time of the murder were Blackstone, Cal Morrow, and Mary Barton. Mary's out, of course, so right now these two guys look like prime suspects."

"Damn it, Bill, we'll need those videos." Ed was getting

tired. He rubbed his forehead and tried to think. "All right, let's seal off this floor and set up the elevator so it won't stop on this floor except with a passkey."

Bill nodded, "Yeah, let's go home."

Soon the crime scene investigation team arrived and began setting up in room 802. The body was carefully removed and carried out of the hotel's back entrance. By now, the zombies were fading away. Activity at The Sylvia Hotel was winding down.

One person, however, remained. Any attempt to play down the incident hadn't fooled this person. She was gathering in everything, and she was good at it. She was Hollywood reporter Brenda Starling.

Monday morning Loren Masters was woken up very early by a call from head office. That was no surprise for her. As Vancouver's Senior Crown Council, this was normal for the hard-working fortyish McGill law grad. But when she answered, it surprised her to hear Chief Blair Bower himself on the line, usually she worked with the Deputy Chief, not the big boss.

"Loren, I'm calling on behalf of the Homicide Department," Blair informed her. "They're working on an important case right now. I'd like you to handle it directly. There was a murder at The Sylvia Hotel last night."

"Wow!" Loren recollected what she'd had heard about the hotel. "Wasn't there some kind of festival over there this weekend; something about a zombie movie?"

"That's right. The victim is R.K. Fielding, president of the big studio that's making the film."

"Uh-oh, famous Oscar-winning producer. That's big. I must talk to Ed right away."

"For sure, and call Forensics; they should have the body in the lab by now."

Loren grabbed The Vancouver Sun from the rack outside Starbucks on her walk to her office. She was looking for early news on the crime. But there was nothing about the murder, only a small article about a disturbance at the hotel. As she sat down with her coffee, she remembered the Chief's request to touch base with the Forensic Investigation Unit. She grabbed up her cell and pushed her pre-set for Dr. Elonzo Francis, Chief Forensic Pathologist.

"Yes, Loren," came the quick reply.

"Elonzo, what do you have so far on The Sylvia Hotel homicide?"

"We're wrapping it up, but I have to tell you now, Loren, this case has a weird twist."

"Twist?" Loren didn't want to hear that. "Okay, tell me."

"Sorry, I can't do that over the phone. Best you come over here; I'll fill you in."

Despite his grueling shifts over the two previous days, Ed Steelside was up before noon and standing out on the sidewalk. Bill swung by to pick him up.

"What's the progress?" Ed asked, settling into the seat.

"The Chief has put Loren on the case. I've sent her what we have, and she's all up to date. She wants to meet over at the forensics lab early. It seems Elonzo wants to discuss the autopsy with us."

"She's an excellent choice," Ed added. "Have we located Blackstone yet?"

"Yeah. The guy left the hotel after he met with RK. He's out at some movie studio in Maple Ridge. His office says you can interview him out there."

"Good God," Ed grimaced. "So, the mountain has to go to Mohamed. Who is this guy? Doesn't he realize he's one step away from jail?"

"He's pretty damn cocky; don't be surprised if he tries to stonewall you."

Ed was now getting jumpy. "We have to move fast; some of our suspects may not be Canadian citizens. I don't want anyone pulling a Polanski on us."

Bill thought of Roman Polanski, the movie director who had skipped out of the United States when charged for child rape back in the '70s.

"Yeah, Blackstone's a US citizen, and so is Morrow!"

Bill swung his car into the parking spot marked Police Only at the Vancouver Police Department's Forensic Investigation Unit. The lab was near St Paul's Hospital in downtown Vancouver. Loren Masters was waiting to meet the two men as they entered the holding area.

"I know very little yet," she informed them. "Elonzo has put a quietus on the autopsy report. We all had to meet here."

A strong aroma of formaldehyde assaulted the group as they entered the examining room. An older, balding man was washing his hands over a basin. He turned and greeted the three people.

"Sorry to be so secretive," Dr. Elonzo Francis mentioned. "This is a strange autopsy. I wanted to brief you here myself and explain our findings before I release my written report."

"That's good," Ed replied, gazing over at a sheet-covered body lying on a steel table. "Until now, only two witnesses, other than us, know the cause of death."

"Well that's our big mystery," Elonzo announced, "that big ugly knife in the victim's head." He pulled back the sheet, revealing the body.

"As you can see, there's an enormous gaping hole in the frontal region of the victim's forehead, exposing some brain matter. After we removed the knife and cleaned the area of penetration," Elonzo held up his closed hand, "we found this embedded in the rear bone structure of the skull." He opened his hand and revealed a small lead bullet.

"You're kidding!" Loren exclaimed. "Are you saying the victim was shot? Not stabbed?"

"Yes. This bullet caused the death. Not the knife. That weapon was employed after the victim was mortally wounded and lying on his back. The entire crime scene was staged!"

The group stood in silence for a moment, trying to reconcile this new turn of events.

"Where's the knife?" Ed broke the ice.

"It's over there," Elonzo pointed to a knife lying on a nearby table.

"Can we get prints off it?"

"No, sorry, Ed, it was clean. Whoever did it must have used gloves."

"Do you have an approximate time of death?" Loren asked.

"Yes. I would place the death at around 11:30 p.m., not much earlier."

"Okay, Elonzo," Ed weighed in. "Go ahead and file your report, but please, let as few people know about this as possible. We need to interview more suspects."

"I'll do my best," the doctor replied. He then placed the sheet back over the body.

It was late Monday afternoon when Ed pulled his car off the Fraser Valley country highway and onto a small gravel road; but it didn't look right. It was the address they had given him, yet the entrance looked more like an unassuming farm road than the gateway to Canada's most prominent movie studio. But as he drove on in, the road opened up into a wide secluded valley, revealing a vast studio complex. Diverse landscapes surrounded the large workshop buildings, offering a movie director any countryside they might dream up for filming.

Ed drove up to the main gate, stopped and presented his ID. The guard directed him towards the UnDead filming location. He parked next to a huge, box-like building and walked to the front entrance. Greeting him in the main lobby was a hand-lettered sign announcing 'Zombies On A Plane.'

Another guard appeared and escorted him to an elevator leading up to an open walkway high above. Ed followed the man along a catwalk that overlooked an impressive movie set below. He could see they had assembled a full-size mock-up of a passenger airliner. The fuselage was cut in half lengthwise, like a big sausage sliced open for a bun. There was a camera up on a clever rail track arrangement, allowing it to pan the exposed cabin's full length.

They arrived at Blackstone's glassed-in office near the end of the walkway. The guard tapped on the door, opened it, and let Ed enter.

Sitting behind a modern teak wood desk was a fiftyish, stylishly dressed man, his back turned to Ed. He was reading what appeared to be a stapled movie script.

"Have a seat," he stated, without turning around.

Ed frowned. He sat in the chair.

The man turned. He had a tanned face, accented by a thin silver mustache.

"Ah, yes. Ed, is it? I understand you have a few questions for me?"

"I have a lot of questions for you," Ed countered, somewhat annoyed. "I want to know of your whereabouts on last Saturday evening?"

"Oh, you're referring to the time of RK's tragic death. I just heard about it this morning. Mary called me with the shocking news, and then this other guy called me, a…"

"Sergeant Doland," Ed reminded him.

"Yes, he mentioned you would like to interview me or something?"

"Sir, let's get right to the point. Exactly where were you from 9:00 p.m. to 2:00 a.m. Saturday night?"

"Well, I had a meeting with RK around 10:00 p.m. We talked about some script changes, then I left him and came out here to the studio."

"Why did you leave the hotel? You had a room there?"

"Mary Barton had booked rooms for all the staff. I guess she didn't know I was coming back here. I needed to be on set early."

"I want you to listen carefully," Ed paused for effect. "Tell me the exact time you left RK's room after you met with him."

"The exact time? Well, I don't know. We talked about a few things; I would say I left RK's room around 10:15, um, 10:20. I can't be sure."

"And at what time did you leave the hotel?"

Blackstone appeared a bit annoyed. "Only 10 minutes later. I had to get my things from my room and get down to the parking garage. Maybe ten more minutes. Why?"

Ed didn't answer. "When you left RK's room, was anyone else on that floor?"

"No. I saw no one."

"I have one last question for you. Did you and RK have any differences, was this meeting purely business?"

"Differences?" Arvin replied, somewhat put off. "What kind of differences?"

"Any animosity between you and him, any disagreements?"

"We're in a highly visible, volatile profession, Detective.

15

We all have our differences. But it has never interfered with our work. We had a good meeting discussing the picture. That's all!"

Ed stood up from the table. He clicked off his cell, hidden in his pocket. "Very well then, that will do for now. But I'm officially informing you now, sir, that you will not leave Canada. Is that clear?"

"I have no problem with that," Arvin replied, as a slight brief smile crept onto his face. "I have a film to complete."

On Ed's evening drive back to Vancouver, his hands-free phone on the car dash buzzed. He voice-commanded it on. "Yeah," he answered.

Bill's voice came on the speaker. "Ed, what's Blackstone saying?"

"He's innocent as a lamb if you believe him. He says he and RK had a business meeting. Then he left around 10:20 and went straight out to the studios."

"Well, I just got a call from Anita Fielding, RK's widow. She just flew in from LA and get this: she's got a whole different story she wants to tell."

"The best news I've heard all day. Is she available now?"

"You bet. This woman is ready to talk. She's staying at the Marriott."

"Great. I'm still out of town, but I can make it there in about an hour. Tell her I'm on the way."

As Ed neared Vancouver on the freeway, he snapped on his car radio just in time to catch the lead story on the six o'clock news…

"Famous motion picture mogul R.K. Fielding was found brutally murdered at The Sylvia Hotel late Saturday night! Police Chief Blair Bower is hush-hush on the case. Reports say the killer is still on the loose and may be part of the crowd celebrating the

making of the UnDead studio's new movie, Zombies On A Plane!

How Fielding was killed is still sketchy; rumors are he may have been slain zombie style! Forces are on the alert. Is there a crazed killer stalking our city? Brenda Starling reporting."

"Bloody hell!" Ed muttered to himself. So much for Elonzo's confidential autopsy.

TV news vans, reporters, and camera crews surrounded the Marriott's immediate area when Ed drove up. He decided it best to go past the hotel, then go down a side street and find a parking spot. If any of the media spotted him, they would be on him like fleas on a hound. Ed parked, then sat and wondered what to do next. Suddenly his cell buzzed. He picked it up immediately.

"Ed Steelside," he answered.

"Ed, this is Anita Fielding. Where are you?"

"I'm parked out on a side street. What's going on?"

Anita's voice was nervous and fearful. "I snuck out of the hotel down the stairwell. I'm walking behind the hotel. Can you pick me up?"

"Got it. Wait. What are you wearing?"

"A yellow coat."

Ed pulled his car back onto the street next to the Marriott and rolled along until he soon spotted a tall, slender woman walking furtively. She had on a short, yellowish jacket. He pulled up beside her, and made a slight hand wave. She noticed, and got into the car.

"Oh my God, what a nightmare!" The woman gasped, slumping back in the seat. "I'm Anita, I hope the hell you're Ed?"

Ed couldn't help but notice the poor woman's frazzled condition. "Not to worry, Anita. I know a quiet little place on Hornby. You look like you could use a drink."

The two people entering Sal's Wine Bar could have been any of the law court professionals who often frequented the little bar next to the Vancouver courts building. They sat at a corner table. The low candlelit lighting tamed the evening for Anita. Her face brightened, she chose a chardonnay and settled her tired frame back into the soft leather.

"Thanks," she approved. "You've saved the day."

"How did the press find you, Anita?"

"I have no idea! When I got to the hotel, they were all camped out in the lobby."

Ed felt he needed to explain somehow. "Anita, I swear to God, neither I nor any of my staff leaked this out. Hell, I didn't even know you were coming until Bill called."

Anita held up her glass. "Welcome to Hollywood, Ed! Such a lovely place. Everybody's on the God damn make."

"Yes, I've got a good dose of that today." Ed clicked on his cellphone, and began what he hoped wouldn't be an uncomfortable interview in a public place.

"First," Ed began, "I want to offer my deepest condolences in the tragic news of your husband's death, especially on such brief notice."

Anita didn't appear to be too shaken. "Don't worry, Roland and I separated years ago; we pretty much led separate lives ever since then."

"Were you still on good terms?"

"Oh, yes. He was a good man; we were happy in the arrangement. It suited us."

Ed felt it was proper now for him to get to the subject. "Anita, you notified us you have some concerns over your husband's relationship with Arvin Blackstone?"

"More than just concerns," Anita answered straight out. "I have a good reason to believe the son-of-a-bitch killed him!"

Ed tried to keep his composure over this sudden revelation.

"Why do you say that?"

Anita set down her glass. She parsed her next words carefully. "Arvin Blackstone worked secretly behind my husband's back, trying to replace him as the president, spreading rumors, sabotaging Roland's projects. Then, just recently, Roland discovered something disturbing about Arvin. He came over to my place, his voice as angry as I've ever heard him. He said he had Arvin good this time, that Arvin was going down big time. He was going to go to the owners with it!"

"Did Roland tell you what that was?"

"No," Anita replied. She set her glass down. "It was the last time I talked to Roland about Blackstone." Anita's voice soon revealed her anguish. "That's the...," she paused to collect her emotions. "That's the last time I ever saw him alive."

Ed clicked off his cell, "Anita, I promise you I will do everything I can to get to the bottom of this. You have my word."

Tuesday morning proved cold and rainy; water rinsed down the sides of the glass in the Vancouver court's meeting room. Assembled at a meeting table were Ed and Loren, plus Sidhu Presh, a scholarly Indian man and Senior Investigator for the Forensics Investigation Unit. With him was his team of experts in criminal science. They were ready to brief everyone on their findings on The Sylvia Hotel murder. Sidhu opened the meeting with a rundown of his search on the 8th floor.

"The carpet around the victim's head was spattered with small blood spots," he began. "The killer was meticulous. We detected no victim's blood in other parts of the room, nor the hall, nor the elevator." Sidhu produced a photo. "The first weapon was a large wooden-handled butcher knife. The bullet that Elonzo later found in the skull came from a .22-caliber handgun; a small weapon easily concealed."

"Sidhu," Loren asked, "how accurate is Elonzo's estimated

time of death?"

Sidhu went to the blackboard. He circled 11:30 p.m. "This is the coroner's approximate time of death. It represents a window of time judged by the body's temperature, food in the stomach, age differences, medications, etc. We can determine that window to be between 11:25 and 11:45 p.m."

"What is your team's rationale on how this crime was carried out?" Loren continued.

"The killer, no doubt, surprised the victim by pulling out a concealed pistol and shooting him point blank in the forehead. The body fell, then the killer positioned it on the floor for better leverage in the stabbing." Sidhu bent down to demonstrate. "The killer placed the knife over the bullet hole with one hand, then with the other, pounded it down with the palm of his hand thusly." Sidhu showed the action. "We know this took a series of mighty hits until the knife went through the skull—going deep into the victim's brain."

"Why wasn't there more blood at the scene?"

"The pathology report noted that although the bullet had killed the victim immediately, the heart would continue to beat. However, there would be little heart activity by the time of the stabbing, which occurred at least 3 to 4 minutes later."

With that, Sidhu set down his notes and concluded his findings. "Most of the evidence we have," he deduced, "gives us a time-line of about 10 minutes for the killer to commit the actual physical part of the killing, then leave. The crime itself suggests a pre-planned murder that required a good deal of thought and preparation."

Loren turned to Ed. "What's your feeling here, Ed? How do you see this scenario?"

"The killer is no dummy, that's for sure," Ed began. "If it was Blackstone, and if he did this alone without an accomplice, he would have to show he left the hotel when RK was still alive. That would be his alibi. Suppose Blackstone returned later, around 11:30, to commit the crime. In that case, he'd need a disguise to avoid being recognized by his staff or being recorded by the security cameras."

"Of course!" Loren realized. "The killer could walk around the hotel during a costumed zombie festival. He could have worn a zombie disguise. He would have fit right into the crowd."

"That's right," Ed added. "That's how I think he did it. He dressed as a zombie and somehow came up to the 8th floor, then back down without being noticed. But the hotel security recordings will show him leaving room 802, and we can follow him to where he parked his car outside the hotel. Hopefully, there, we can get a positive ID on him."

Loren took a piece of chalk and circled 10:00 p.m. and 11:30 p.m. "Okay then, Ed, we need those damn security recordings. I think it's time we pressure the hotel. They've had enough time now."

As they prepared to leave the room, Ed turned to Loren. "What bothers me most about this," Ed reminded her, "is, if Blackstone is our killer, then he is so twisted, he thought of a way to use RK's body as a promotion for his new movie. That's the kind of perverse creep we're dealing with here."

It was midday when the sky, at last, broke clear over Vancouver. The clouds had withdrawn, and the sun had made its appearance—treating the day's drivers with gleaming harbors and clear blue peaks framing the northern shore. These are the delightful, reassuring sights that happen now and then in the city, helping to remind Vancouverites why they live in this crowded place, jammed in like cattle in a chute along the car-packed streets.

But on this day, they were also treated to some titillating revelations from their car radios, providing them with some juicy Hollywood intrigue.

"UnDead Movie Producer's secretary Mary Barton discovered her boss mysteriously murdered. Why are the Police hiding the gory evidence of a zombie-style killing? Is the Forensics Lab in a cover-up? What are they hiding?

Why is Police Detective Ed Steelside stymied in finding the killer? Reports are Steelside brutally manhandled a zombie fan at The Sylvia Hotel, asking: What strange event took place in Room 802?

Reports are the slain movie mogul's wife is hiding, what does she know? Why is Crown Prosecutor Loren Masters still not talking?

-Brenda Starling with a special report. More news at 11:00."

A call came in at Ed's police precinct on Broadway. It was from Darin Lawson, over at The Sylvia Hotel. Bill grabbed it. "Darin, what's up?"

"I've got good news, Bill. The hotel's owners have granted you total access to our security recordings. They want to cooperate fully with the Police. Sorry for the wait!"

"Alright, Darin, this is great news. Send them straight to our crime lab on Hastings."

It was around two in the afternoon when Loren met with Ed and Bill at the Technical Investigation Lab.

Bill was the most excited. "I've got the Maple Ridge RCMP on alert," he announced. "They're ready to haul in Blackstone's ass within a minute's notice."

The group assembled outside the video suite. The facility's young, head technician, Andy Carver, was there to usher them in. They sat, and Andy brought up the video coverage of the 8th Floor, the elevator in the foreground and 802, RK's room, down the hall. Andy started the video rolling, the recording time clicking away at the bottom of the screen.

The video ran motionless until the first movement occurred—the elevator door opened, and RK stepped out with Blackstone behind him. They entered 802 and shut the door. *-10:26 p.m.*

"Can you speed it up?" Loren requested. Andy fast-forwarded until 802's door re-opened. Blackstone stepped out, shut the door and entered the elevator. *-10:32 p.m.*

"Run it on, Andy!" Loren was betraying her impatience. Andy sped up the view and 17 minutes elapsed before another movement occurred. "Stop!" Loren shouted.

There on the screen was Cal Morrow, entering the hallway from his room! He proceeded to room 802, knocked, and entered. *-11:04 p.m.*

"Christ Almighty," Bill stammered. "That lying bastard!"

Loren was beside herself. She looked over at Ed. "What the hell just happened?"

"Let's see when he comes out," Ed answered, somewhat perplexed. "That's the key."

Andy sped up the motion until 802's door opened. Cal stepped out. "Freeze it!" Ed ordered. He began staring intently at the image. "Can you sharpen it?" he asked.

"Not much, Ed. It's not hi-res."

"What are you looking for?" Loren questioned.

"Blood specks, a sign of the gun," Ed replied. "Something Cal shouldn't have if he's not the killer." Ed studied the screen intently; then he shook his head. "Okay, run it on."

Andy started the video—Cal returned to his room, entered and shut the door. *-11:23 p.m.*

"We're near the time of death," Loren noted. "My God, Ed did Cal do it?"

"We still have time left for a killer," Ed noted. "Let's see if our zombie shows up."

Andy sped the motion on until the elevator finally opened. Mary Barton emerged. She walked down the hallway, entered her room, shut the door. *-12:37 a.m.*

Andy sped the film until Mary returned to the hallway. She went over to RK's room; the meds were probably in her pocket. She knocked, then entered. *-1:03 a.m.*

"That's enough," Ed exclaimed, frustrated. "We're out of it now. The show's over!"

Loren turned to her teammates. "Well, I guess there's no other conclusion," she announced to the startled group. "Unless our killer is the invisible man, I'm afraid Cal Morrow is the last person to see RK Fielding alive!"

"All right then," Ed resigned himself. "Let's not wait any longer." He turned to Bill. "Go ahead and bring Cal in."

The late Tuesday rush hour in downtown traffic was something to be avoided. But it didn't seem to matter for the two detectives stranded on the expressway. Ed and Bill sat discouraged in their slow-moving, unmarked car. The case they were building was now a derailed train, flung off into a deep ravine, scattering pieces everywhere. They needed to start over. But they didn't know what pieces to pick up to get back on the rails.

"Why?" Bill uttered to Ed, sitting beside him. "Why did Cal do it? He knew he'd be recorded going into that room. What was his motive? Why the knife scenario? Did he lose it and think he was a character in one of his freaking movie scripts?"

Ed pondered the question. "The only thing that makes any sense, Bill, is that Cal didn't know RK was dead when I interviewed him. That's why he didn't think it was a big deal when he lied to us about seeing RK or entering his room. Blackstone did it Bill, I'm sure of it."

"Sorry, Ed, we have nothing else now to go on. We have to face this. Cal did it!"

"We need to meet with Sidhu again, Bill. Let's go over the crime scene one more time."

Bill shook his head. "You're the boss, Ed, but Loren's filing charges against Cal in the morning, and unless we put Blackstone in that hotel room, this case is closed."

Ed was at the city lock-up late that evening for the official interrogation of the prisoner. Cal was already seated in the small holding room when he entered. Ed sat across from him. The man he had interviewed Saturday night was young, strong and confident. But the man he saw today looked 20 years older, his face sickly pale and withdrawn. Ed looked him straight in the eye and began.

"Cal, when I last talked to you, you said you never met with RK that night. Now I know you were lying to me."

"Yes, I said that," Cal answered directly. "I was trying to protect RK."

"But RK was dead then. How could you protect him?"

"I didn't know he was dead when you were questioning me. When you told me that, I was so shocked, I didn't know what to do. I just sat down, tried to clear my head."

"Why not tell me the truth after you found out?"

"I was still confused. When I had come up to my room earlier, I was woozy. I had lain down. But I remembered RK told me he wanted me to meet with him around 11:00. I was late, but I went over. That's when he told me no one was to know about our meeting."

"What was the meeting about?"

"RK told me he had just fired Blackstone—I was to take his position. He told me Arvin had threatened him, and he must be careful, not let anyone know of his next plan."

"And that was?"

"To expose Arvin for wrongdoing."

Ed thought of widow Anita Fielding's accusation. It was almost exactly what she had said about Blackstone. "Cal, you had two days to come forward and tell the truth. Surely you knew you would be accused by now."

"No!" Cal's voice was becoming more distressed, "I had no reason to believe that because I didn't do it! Blackstone must have killed RK, but I don't understand it. Why wasn't there any proof showing him going into RK's room? RK was alive when I left. Why? Why didn't that become revealed?"

Cal was now in total distress. He put his head down on the table. He was done.

Wednesday's morning sun didn't seem as cheerful as Tuesday's sun to Ed. It was still out, the mountains again clear, but the atmosphere in his office was now dreary. Nobody in his team liked the thought of Blackstone getting off, but they moved on. There were still many bad people out there, suspicious deaths to investigate, dead or missing loved ones to find. They accepted it, and moved on.

Then, The Sylvia Hotel called.

"Ed, it's Bruce in Security. Guess what we found?"

A glimmer of hope flashed in Ed's mind. "I'm listening!"

"One of our hotel maids found a gun in room 802!"

"No, shit, where?"

"It was hidden in the toilet tank. Isn't that wild?"

But when Bruce clicked off, Ed's heart sank. The missing gun was Cal's last chance for innocence. Since the killer had left the gun there, now that alibi was gone.

Loren had started her prosecution of Cal Morrow, even though Ed had called for another post-crime scene meeting. All evidence was in now, but Loren had agreed to another sit-down. They had set the time at 1:00 p.m. that afternoon. Ed, Bill, and Sidhu Presh were present. Andy Carver from the video lab was also there for his technical expertise.

Sidhu stood up and started the meeting. "First off," he began, "the gun used in the crime is a .22-caliber Smith and Wesson handgun, but the serial number has been filed off, so that's a dead end."

"Sidhu, what about the gun and the knife together?" Loren asked. "How did they get into the room?"

"I'll let Andy address that," he replied.

Andy passed some printouts from the security video around the table. "As you can see here," Andy noted, "the briefcase Cal is carrying is a standard 14-inch size. The butcher knife is 12 inches. It could easily fit with the gun beside it."

"Andy," Loren asked again, "could someone have tampered with any of these video recordings—altered them in any way?"

"Loren, the answer to that is no, not in any way possible without detection. It's true that with sophisticated equipment, it's conceivable to hack into a security system, but it would be easily spotted. Plus, it would be impossible to alter the time readouts embedded in the code. It's synced with the digital; that would show up as a hack in the system as well."

Loren turned to Sidhu. She wanted a scenario for all the latest information. "Sidhu, how do you see this crime acting out now based on these accurate timelines?"

Sidhu went to the chalkboard. He circled 11:30 p.m. as the approximate time of death. "We know Cal entered the room at 11:04. We believe he had a heated conversation with RK regarding his position at the studio. Cal alleges RK said he would be the new head producer and replace Blackstone. But if that were true, why would he kill RK? We could say the opposite is true. He was told he was fired! That could be a plausible motive."

Ed had a question now. "What's your best timeline for the actual killing?"

"I believe that at around 11:10, Cal opened his briefcase,

took out the gun, and shot RK in the head. He still would have enough time to stage the body with the knife, then leave the room at 11:23. When Cal didn't open his door after it was banged on, he claimed he was feeling woozy. But that could have been a stalling excuse, giving him time to make sure he cleared his room of any evidence."

"Yes, but Sidhu," Loren added, "why would Cal stage a phony knife scene?"

"All I can say to that," Sidhu allowed, "is this is a writer's fantasy creation, a zombie killing. Maybe he was obsessed with that—who knows? To commit an act like this is disturbing. Maybe he flipped? That would explain why he lied, and earlier, his denial of even being there."

Ed had another question. "The time of death was early by 19 minutes. Is that a factor in questioning the time?"

"I asked Dr. Francis if he thinks that is reasonable. The time of death estimation is a bit early but still flexible enough to fit."

"In that case," Ed added, "the window could stretch out to a later time for the victim to have been killed, say even 20 minutes later, should someone else have come into the room?"

"Yes, Ed, but of course, no one did."

"Just one last thing, Sidhu," Loren asked. "Is that hotel room secure? Could anyone have gotten into it, other than through the door?"

"Good question, Loren. I was coming to that. We went over that room totally. The windows are sealed; it's on the 8th floor with no access from the outside. They built this hotel like a fortress; it's old-style technology, but it's solid. No one could get into that room except by the door. We can only conclude that Cal Morrow was the last person to be in that room at the time of the murder and that he alone is the killer."

Loren looked over to Ed. She felt she should let him

comment. "Ed, what would you like to add to this report?"

Ed frowned. He rubbed his forehead. "I still have many concerns about this case. We have serious conflicting statements from Arvin Blackstone's associates about his involvement with the deceased. Many statements cause me to doubt Blackstone's honesty. But, as of now, I have no other evidence to contradict the findings. So, I have to agree with the final analysis."

Ed closed his notebook and slumped back in his chair. He had to hand it to Presh. The man's argument made sense. It fit everything.

Loren stood up. She gave Ed an apologetic glance. "It is concluded then," she said reluctantly, "that there is sufficient evidence for the Crown Prosecutor's office to proceed with the charge of first-degree murder against Cal Morrow."

The evening news broadcast that night was getting interesting. Now there were some more titillating disclosures for the masses…

"Breaking News! We have just learned Associate Producer and Screen Writer Cal Morrow has been officially charged with first-degree murder of his boss, R.K. Fielding.

What do we know about this man's secret life? Did he act out his horrifying script for a zombie-style killing? Morrow is the writer who coined the phrase, 'Zombies always come back!'

Rumors are he brutally murdered his boss because he was flipping out from a depraved lifestyle. Did he plan to take over the studio? What do we really know of the secret goings-on and the sordid dealings of Hollywood movie elite?

Freelance reporter Brenda Starling live on the scene at the courthouse."

Mary Barton's voice was upset when she called Ed that evening. "These news reports on Cal are wrong," she began.

"RK would never fire Cal. He needed Cal. He was the most important writer on the team. These are all lies. Lies!"

"We know that, Mary. We are doing everything we can," he reassured her.

"It's too late now, Ed," she added. "The board has appointed Arvin CEO. He's taken over the entire shoot. He's changed direction; overturned everything RK had worked for."

After Mary hung up, Ed couldn't help but wonder what else he could find? He went over to Bill's desk. "Is there anything new on the video search over at the crime lab?" he asked.

"No, Ed, it's a dead issue now. Andy will wrap it up today."

That evening, Ed was about to sign off work and go home when his cell buzzed. It was Andy, over at the tech lab. Ed quickly grabbed it up.

"Yeah, Andy, what's up?"

"I've been watching the UnDead group downstairs, Ed— you know, when they were all at the party table. I noticed something suspicious. I think Blackstone secretly dropped something in Cal's glass. It's subtle, but it's there. It looks like a small pill or something."

"Of course, that's it," Ed replied. "That would explain Cal's strange behavior; it was probably a strong hallucinogenic. Cal wouldn't have known what hit him. Great work Andy.

Thursday marked five days from the time of The Sylvia Hotel murder. Ed was getting depressed. He still had the usual shooting or robbery investigations that filed across his desk. These were routine crimes. The perpetrator was arrested, the information gathered, witness testimonies all meticulously recorded and filed. But the Sylvia murder was left open, unfinished, and unsolved. He could not let it go.

Ed decided he needed a place to think when the noon

hour rolled around. He left the office and walked over to the local bus stop to catch the 15-minute bus ride to English Bay. Ed got off close to The Sylvia and stopped at a little deli. He bought himself a chicken wrap, then proceeded on towards the The Sylvia Hotel.

There he found a shady little park bench close to the hotel. He took out his sandwich and sat, studying the old building. It had no outside fire escapes. It was a structure built ahead of its time, with internal stairwells.

He considered the ivy vines entwined around and up the side of the building. Could someone have climbed up those vines and reached the 8th-floor windows? No. It was impossible. He had examined all those windows himself. They were all tightly locked. Plus, the hotel was lit up at night—any Spiderman crawling up the side would be instantly seen.

He sat gazing, trying to think. What was he missing? But nothing was coming. Yet somehow, it helped to be here, close to the mystery.

Soon an elderly man came walking up to the park's little fountain. He began hand-feeding some tiny wrens that had gathered by the water. The old fellow seemed in total serenity with the bubbling fountain and the quiet peeping of the scurrying birds. The man walked to the other side. Then he noticed Ed watching him.

"I feed 'em every day," he mentioned to Ed. "I've always enjoyed coming here to visit The Sylvia. It brings back a lot of memories for me."

"Have you been living in this area long?" Ed inquired.

"All my life; she's my gal," he answered, nodding towards the hotel as if it was human.

Ed noticed the man was dressed in a suit and tie for a casual stroll, but he knew this was normal for people from older times. Back in their day, they never went out in public casually dressed.

"You talk as if you know The Sylvia well," Ed noted, somewhat intrigued.

"Oh, I sure do—worked here for almost 60 years."

"That so," Ed replied. Now he was curious. He arose and walked over to the fountain.

"I'm Ed Steelside," he introduced himself, holding out his hand. The man shifted his cane to his other hand, tottering a bit for support, and accepted the handshake.

"Willy McTavish," he replied.

"Willy, you must have some interesting stories about this old building?"

"Oh yeah. I went to work here in 1936 when I was 16," he replied with a wry grin. "Told 'em I was 18, but I looked older, so they hired me. I started as a janitor, then a doorman, and finally, baggage porter. Had that job when I retired."

"Wow, that's a lot of history. Tell me about it?"

"How much time you got?" Willy smiled.

"I've got all noon," Ed answered, pointing over to the bench.

Willy settled into the bench's seat while Ed held his cane and little sack of birdseed. Willy flashed him a smile. "Thank you," he said. "You know I meet lots of people here, but nobody's ever got any time to talk anymore. They rush, rush. What the hell's their hurry?"

"Not me," Ed assured him. "Tell me, why do you call the Sylvia your girl?"

"She's a lady to me—grand, elegant, a proper mistress. There was nothing like her." Willy had to pause for a minute. "Yes, for sure, just about every famous person who came to this town stayed here back then. Clark Gable, Errol Flynn, Lana Turner—I met them all when they came through that door."

This revelation floored Ed; he was fascinated with this

man's intriguing life story. "Who were your favorites, Willy?" he asked him.

"Oh God, that's a tough one! Bob Hope gave me the biggest tips; Crosby was a proper gentleman. But you know that cheapskate Howard Hughes never tipped me a dime!"

"Hughes?" Ed responded. "Did he stay here? I always thought he had stayed at the Bayshore."

"Oh, Hughes stayed at the Sylvia a year before he stayed at the Bay," Willy reflected. "Around 1962, I think. The Sylvia didn't want that kind of attention then, and neither did Howard."

"How long did he stay here?"

"I'd say 7 or 8 months; he rented out the entire top floor. At one time, that floor was a restaurant, but it was converted to penthouses just before Hughes took it. Nobody else could go up there but Hughes."

"8th floor?" Ed responded, getting very interested.

"Yes, he used the biggest suite there, room 802."

Ed almost fell off his seat. He tried not to sound too excited. "Tell me all about that."

"Well, the rumor-mill had it that Hughes was secretly having liaisons with various movie starlets: Jane Russell, Lana Turner. But whenever those actresses visited, I always took their baggage to the 7th floor. They'd have their rooms there."

"Did you ever take anybody up to the 8th?"

"No, not possible, that floor was always locked off. Movie stars came and went, but it didn't matter how famous they were, nobody was allowed up there. Hughes rarely left that floor, even had his meals brought up by his personal butler. So, I think that's all those rumors were, Ed, just rumors."

"Willy, can I get your phone number? I'd like to talk to you some more about this."

"Sure, but I don't have a phone, Ed. I'm staying at a care

facility, but I have their card. You can find me there just about any time."

Ed took Willy's card and shook the man's hand. "Willy, here's my card; I'm a detective. I want to thank you. We'll talk again."

As Ed walked back to the bus, he reflected on the unbelievable coincidence of this chance meeting with Willy. It was a long shot, but it was the most significant lead he'd had to date.

Bill was back from lunch and had just settled into his routine when Ed came rushing in the door. He threw his coat on a chair. "Bill, call Andy," he exclaimed as he hurried down the hall. "My office now!"

"Alright, what's up?"

"We've been watching the wrong floor," Ed barked. "We should watch the 7th floor!"

Bill reached Andy and put him on the speakerphone. "Andy, I'm in Ed's office. Ed's got some news; I don't know what's going on, but listen up."

"Okay, you guys, new direction," Ed started. "Andy, you eyeball videos on the room directly below, probably 702, on the 7th floor. I want to see everything in that room—who's in, who's out. Follow the last person to leave that room on Saturday night, no matter where they go."

"Okay, I'm on it now."

Ed then turned to Bill. "Ring up that Sylvia manager again, Darin Lawson. Tell him I want to know who booked the rooms directly below 802 on the 7th floor for Saturday night. Ask him if I can get complete floor plan drawings of those two floors. Also, notify Sidhu, have him bring in the electronics surveillance team again. I want another scan of that room looking for additional evidence."

"You want to tell me what the hell's going on, Ed?"

"Just a hunch, Bill, that's all."

Around 3 p.m., Loren called Ed, and she was a bit agitated. Ed dreaded the call; he knew what was coming. "Yes, Loren,"

"Ed, I just heard you're still trying to go after Blackstone. C'mon Ed, I've got to build a case now," she reminded him. "Everything you're sending me is helping Cal's defense. Please try to find something that's helping me out."

"Loren, I've got a new lead. I think it's good. Give me some more time."

"Time for what?" Her voice was not so friendly now. "Come on, Ed. You can't change reality. Cal did it. Yes, Blackstone's a jerk, but he didn't do it—dammit, he wasn't there!" She hung up.

It wasn't long before hotel manager Darin Lawson called back from The Sylvia. Bill put him on speakerphone.

"Sorry, gentlemen," Darin began, "Room 702, below 802, is booked for the long weekend. The whole hotel's full up for months. This case has made us more famous than we would like. As to who booked the rooms for the zombie festival, they were all reserved a month ago by Mary Barton. Two additional rooms on the 7th floor, were booked as back up for guests. However both were never used. So they were empty that night. Now, for those old file records you asked for, all we have are some old accounting boxes in the basement."

"Alright, thanks, Darin. We'll be over to have a look."

Ed shook his head. "Blackstone told Mary what rooms to book. Damn it; the guy controlled everything. We can't pin him down, all we can do is watch those rooms."

"Listen, Ed," Bill demanded, "If I'm going to work with you, I need some answers. What's going on with room 702? And no bullshit this time!"

"I'll explain on the way over to the hotel."

As the two detectives drove through the mid-afternoon

traffic, Bill heard about Ed's encounter with the old-timer at the park. Ed was emphatic in his narrative. "He was there during those days," Ed exclaimed. "He saw it all, lived it all. It all fits."

"Really?" Bill began. "C'mon Ed; you're relying on some old coot you just met on your lunch break? True, he may have worked there, but sorry, Ed, there are so many feathers missing in your theory. It can't fly. I'll give you ten to one all day long, any amount."

"Save that for when you buy all the beer," Ed challenged. "I'll pick the pub."

Manager Darin Lawson greeted the two detectives at the front desk of The Sylvia. "There are some difficulties with your request for the hotel floor plans," he informed them. "We have lost them from that far back. Many people have owned the hotel over the last hundred years. But as I mentioned, we have some old invoices from work done back then. It's in the basement storage. You can take a look."

The old building's basement proved to be a sharp contrast to the hotel's elegant decor above. Large exposed oak beams crossed the ceiling, framing a dark catacomb-like cellar, where piles of discarded old furniture lingered. At the back, against a stone wall, sat a neglected pile of dust-covered accounting files stacked ceiling high.

"Here's what's left of the old records," Darin noted. "Sorry, this is all we have."

Bill tried to lift one box, but it tore from its weight. "This will take time," he groaned, setting the box back down. "What are we looking for?"

"Something that shows money paid for contract work to modify room 802," Ed answered. "The date would start from late 1961 through 1962."

"Alright, I'll ask Sidhu to get a forensic records team down here right away."

"Good, let's get that started." Ed then turned to Darin. "I'd like to go up to your office now, there are some things I'd like to discuss with you privately about 802."

"I was just about to ask you about that," Darin said. "Can you release 802 now? We're into our busy season. We need it back."

"Not yet, Darin. What I have to ask you may affect your hotel's history."

Darin ushered Ed into his office and shut the door. "Would you care to explain what you're getting to, Ed?" he asked nervously.

"Tell me about this hotel's background," Ed pressed him. "I'm interested in the early 1960's. Did Howard Hughes ever rent the entire top floor?"

Darin sat perplexed for a moment, trying to fathom Ed's request. "I can't answer that. The hotel was owned by the Saw-yer family back then. We inherited very few hotel records from those days. I've heard the story about Hughes; it has some merit. Sawyer's daughter Jill Davie hinted in her memoirs about Hughes staying here, but what does this have to do with the murder?"

"Darin, I believe Hughes may have done some secret ren-ovation work to his room before he moved in." Ed carefully framed his next words. "Hotel building codes may not have approved those modifications, nor were they done with the hotel owner's knowledge."

Darin's immediate reaction was to challenge the detective. But, he hesitated, to weigh the accusation carefully. "Okay, just what are you implying?"

"I think Hughes included room 702, which is directly below 802, in his rental agreement. Then he modified it to allow him access to it."

"Do you have any proof of this?"

"This is just between you and me, Darin. I don't have proof yet, but I have a good source. As to any illegal doings, it may not have been unlawful since Hughes gave occupants knowledge of that access and the pass key to anyone using it."

"Okay, I get it. You're suggesting that Hughes was setting up a situation to bring movie starlets up to his room undetected for sexual encounters, some kind of hidden passageway?"

"Yes, but Hughes probably thought no one would ever find it. I'm sure he threw away the key, but I think someone else has found it, and that's why I'm here."

"Ed, I hope the hell you're wrong about this."

"I hope the hell I'm right," Ed countered back. "A man's freedom is on the line."

The day was now getting late as the two detectives drove back to the station. Soon they came up to a red light. As they sat waiting for the green, a city bus pulled up beside them. Displayed on its side, a garish movie poster depicting an airline pilot walking up a boarding ramp. Peering out from under the captain's visor-two-evil red eyes glaring menacingly from a rotting zombie face. The copy emblazoned across the top—*Your Flight Will Depart Soon!*

Friday morning, The Sylvia Hotel was a busy place. But it wasn't the kind of busyness that Darin wanted. Technicians had set up scanning equipment on the 8th floor. Sidhu Presh had brought up his special surveillance unit for an x-ray examination to test the floor and walls. Another specialist team was sifting through the files in the basement, pouring through stacks of yellowed documents. CSI tape barriers were strung everywhere around both floors.

Ed and Bill decided they would sit and wait back at the

station. Hopefully, by the end of the day, something would happen. But it wasn't from the hotel the first call came. It was from Andy.

Bill put him on a speakerphone in Ed's office. "Yeah, Andy, what have you got?"

Andy's voice was hesitant. "Sorry, guys," he told them, "but I've eyed these videos over and over, and it's a negative."

"What do you mean it's negative?" Ed responded. "Who entered room 702 that night?"

"No one," Andy replied. "Not one person came or left that room the entire night. Lots of zombies filed by, but nobody, zombie or else, entered that room."

Ed leaned back in his chair, total exasperation on his face.

"Okay, Andy. Thanks for your time."

It was around 4 pm when Ed and Bill got the last call from Sidhu. Bill quickly put him on a speakerphone in Ed's office.

"Okay, guys," Sidhu began, "here's what we have. We've radar scanned room 802 completely, but we have detected no space readings inside the wall structure. The mahogany panels were also tested, but we found no device that might act as a key opening or latch. The laser scans show the panels are flush to a solid wall, no chance of any way through them."

"What about the flooring," Bill added, "any possibility it could have been cut through?"

"Bill, our scan analysis of the floor shows 2 inches of solid oak. Underneath that, another layer of hard maple. Yes, it could be cut through, but it would take one hell of a sawing job. Plus, the noise would have been too noticeable and lengthy to be done covertly. There's no way through that floor. Sorry, Ed, that's about it."

"Okay, then. How about the historical records search in the basement, anything there?"

"Not much, Ed. Most of the former work done on the hotel

39

was by Campbell & Whipple construction. Their records show they removed the restaurant and restored the rooms on the 8th floor. But they completed this work about six months before Hughes arrived. We found one lone receipt. It showed reno work performed later on the 8th-floor area by a guy named Antonio Bizzaro. Still, it has little info. I'll send it over. Do you still want us to search 702?"

"No, we can forget that now," Ed gloomily noted. "Thank the team for their hard work."

It was late in the afternoon when Ed returned from his meeting with Police Chief Blair Bower. Bill dropped by his office when he came in.

"Looks like everyone wants a piece of our ass, Ed. The accounting office isn't happy about the cost overruns of Sidhu's search."

"They will all have to get in line, Bill. The Chief just gave me the, *you shit head speech*. Any good news at all?"

"Not much. All we got now is this old invoice Sidhu mentioned." He handed it to Ed. "It's a bill for work done in the hotel's area that used to be the kitchen."

Ed opened the fragile piece of paper and read its contents.

"It says here some guy named Antonio Bizzaro removed a cabinet from a closet and filled in the wall. Where would that be in the hotel?"

"Somewhere on the top floor. There used to be a restaurant up there, but unfortunately, we have no floor plans from that time to find out where it was."

"There's one guy who know's" Ed replied. "Here's his card."

Willy was in the seniors' center dayroom when the nurse ushered the two detectives inside. She spotted Willy sitting alone.

"Willy," she announced to the room, "you have visitors!" All eyes looked at the two detectives approaching.

"Ed!" Willy called out, excited to see his recently found friend. "I knew you'd come. I told everybody about you, but of course, they didn't believe me."

"I didn't forget about you, Willy, and I've brought my partner along with me; this is Deputy Inspector Bill Doland."

Bill stuck out his hand. "Very glad to meet you, Willy. I've heard a lot about you."

Ed sat down next to Willy. "I'm wondering if you can tell me more about The Sylvia's top floor when it was still a restaurant; where the kitchen was, things like that?"

"I got a scrapbook back in my room, Ed. Let's go look."

Upon entering Willy's small apartment, Ed noticed that tacked on his wallboard were various mementos and photos of the little things that were an essential part of the man's life. Most were yellowed and faded, but were placed with loving care in their proper order.

Willy pulled out a drawer in his dresser and produced a tattered old scrapbook. Inside it were some timeworn pictures from his past.

"My wife passed away many years ago," he revealed. "We never had children. I left my parents back in the old country; I've no other relatives. They're all gone now. The Sylvia helped me find this place when I retired."

It struck Ed how alone Willy was. No wonder he walked to The Sylvia every day. It was all that remained of his past existence.

Bill noticed a sepia-tinted hotel brochure tucked inside the pages of Willie's scrapbook.

"Well, there's an oldie," he observed. "Can I look at that?"

"Sure, Bill. I got that when I first started working there back in 1936."

Bill started reading the brochure out loud. "It says here each room had the use of a modern vacuum cleaner. There were special arrangements for guests' clothes to be washed and dried. Each floor had its own individual dumb waiter that went directly up to the kitchen."

"Oh yeah," Willy added, "The Sylvia was the snazziest hotel in Canada, a real first."

"Wait a minute here!" Bill suddenly realized what he had just said. "Did I just read that the hotel had dumb waiters?" He looked over at Ed.

"Willy, is that true?" Ed questioned. "Each floor had a private dumb-waiter shaft to the kitchen?"

"Sure enough, Ed. But they closed them all off when they moved the kitchen to the first floor."

"How did they close them off?"

"Well, that was pretty darn clever; they just removed the food window, filled in the top and bottom floor, and added a door to make it a little closet."

"Willy," Bill asked, "was that elevator shaft big enough to climb into?"

"Oh, just big enough to squeeze into, I guess. But heck, Bill, nobody had to! They lowered the food down to you and pulled the dirty dishes back up."

By now, Ed was trying to control his excitement. "Willy, where was the restaurant kitchen on the top floor?"

"Right where room 802 is now, Ed; that room replaced the kitchen."

Ed grabbed Willy and gave him a big hug. "Willy, I'm buying you a steak dinner!"

"Gee, Ed, you don't have to do that," Willy reacted, totally surprised. "A hot dog'll do."

"Okay," Ed pondered on the drive back, "there's no

use sending Sidhu back over to try to locate a dumb waiter shaft until we find out more about the work done on that receipt."

"But there's no address on it," Bill noted. "Just a name."

"Yes. Antonio Bizzaro. And a brief description of some work done on a closet for $1,650. There's a number scribbled on the back, *12 24 05,* but if it's a date, it's wrong. That must be a mistake."

"Yeah, strange," Bill surmised. "It's almost as if it made its way to the files by accident."

Ed thought for a while. The one question he kept asking himself came to mind.

"Bill, how do you think Blackstone figured this all out?"

"That's the mystery that's been bugging me," Bill countered. "Obviously, he had a different route."

"Yes, that's what I'm thinking. Maybe we follow Blackstone's trail. Let's call Mary Barton. We'll try to start from that end."

When they arrived back at the precinct, Ed settled into his office chair and keyed in Mary Barton's number at UnDead studios. Hopefully, she was working late. She answered.

"Mary, it's Ed. I need your help. Does the name Antonio Bizzaro sound familiar to you?"

"I certainly shouldn't forget a name like that. How would it concern us?"

"I have no idea; all we know is he's a carpenter from years back."

Mary reflected a bit. "I'll check everything we have. Who would he have contacted here?"

"I have no reference, but not a word of this to Arvin."

"Oh, Ed. I guess I should tell you, Arvin's flying back to LA early Monday morning."

"What! Mary, when did you hear this?"

"He told me this today, but I'm not going with him. I can't stand working for the man. I'm putting in my resignation Monday."

"All right, Mary. Thanks for telling me."

"You gotta be shitting me!" Bill exclaimed, tossing his pen on his desk. He leaned back, letting out a long sigh. "Leaving Monday morning? Good God, what the hell now?"

"We need everyone on board as soon as possible, Bill. We need a plan."

"There's no plan now, Ed. We're going into the long weekend. We're out of time."

"We can't give up now, we're so close. We can do it."

Bill glanced over his notes. "Okay," he resigned himself. "I'll try to get Andy to agree on watching more videos. I'll call him tomorrow; too late to reach him now."

"How about Sidhu?"

"It would break union rules to force his crew to work on a long weekend. But if I can reach him, maybe he'll work on his own."

"Our best worst-case scenario," Ed concluded, "is that we are able to extradite Blackstone back to Canada. We can forget about canceling his passport now. Let's just proceed as if we'll solve this case before Monday morning."

"Alright, I'll tell the hotel we'll need room 802 over the weekend. Luckily, we still have that."

Ed thought of the old receipt. "We also have this Antonio Bizzaro guy."

"Sorry, Ed, but I'm having no luck finding a Bizzaro at any address."

"Maybe his name is fake. Hughes could have paid cash; that would cover his tracks."

"Cash was certainly no problem for Hughes," Bill reflected. "I once read he bought an entire TV station, just so they'd keep showing his favorite movies. But more than likely, Hughes's assistant, a guy named Gordon Margolis, took care of Hughes's personal work. Unfortunately, he died some years ago."

Ed looked at the old receipt again. "Bill, when Sidhu's team was going through those old boxes, he mentioned a business name for old reno work. What was it again?"

Bill checked his notes. "It was Campbell and Whipple, but their work was on the wrong date; that's why we disregarded it. I'll call them. Maybe the name Bizzaro will ring a bell. It's a long shot. Maybe he worked for them at some time."

Saturday morning was the first day of the long weekend. Still, it was not a good day for work at the precinct. A demonstration was going on in Stanley Park, something about tree removals along pathways, and officers were needed for riot control. Police would be short-handed, so Bill had to go over and help out. By 2:00 p.m., however, the park protest had faded, and Bill was heading back to the precinct when his cell buzzed. He could see it was Sidhu. He pulled over and answered.

"Sidhu. I'm so glad I reached you."

"Bill, dammit! Why do you want me to go back into The Sylvia again?" Sidhu was clearly frustrated. "We've scoured it thoroughly. I can't bring my people back now, we're into overtime, and they've gone for the weekend anyway."

"First of all, Sidhu, we have recently found new information; we think there's a way through that floor for sure. Plus, Blackstone is leaving Monday. We want to nail him this weekend."

"All right, I'm listening."

"Ed can be there to help you. We can set up early on Sunday morning. Are we good?"

"We're good, but I hope the hell you're right on this. You guys are wearing out your welcome."

It was late afternoon when Ed's phone buzzed; he glanced at his cell's readout. It was the Campbell and Whipple Construction Company on the line. "Detective Steelside here," he quickly answered.

"Yes, Ed, this is Paul Gilbert, Vice President of Personnel. I understand, sir, that you have requested some information concerning the name Antonio Bizarro."

"Thanks for calling, Paul. Yes! I would like to have any background you have on this man."

Paul cleared his throat. "This was an ex-employee who was terminated almost 50 years ago. The name was a pseudonym. His actual name was Robert James. It took me some time to find his records. It looks like we released him because of the work he performed without company knowledge."

"What kind of work, Paul?"

"Improper renovations that violated code laws, that sort of thing. He was using a fake name for his own personal client work, without our knowledge." Paul rustled some papers. "They listed his last known contact at an unknown location in Langley in 1981. I have no address, but I have a number. I'll send it to your cell."

The number soon flashed up on Ed's screen. He clicked on it, and in a moment an older woman came on the line. "Langley Garden Apartments," she said, her voice slow and unsteady.

"Yes, I'm looking for an Antonio Bizarro or Robert James. Is he living at this address?"

"Oh my goodness, there's no Antonio here. But I'm afraid Bob James passed away years ago."

"I'm sorry to hear that, ma'am. My apologies for bothering you." Ed clicked off. He turned to Bill. "Dead-end there."

Tim Horton's was just across the street from the police station. It had been the Saturday noon hour hangout for the two detectives for years, but it was doing double duty this late evening. Bill got his usual sandwich and Diet Coke. All Ed wanted was coffee and an apple fritter. They sat in the corner.

"Ed, aren't you married yet?" Bill asked, coming right out of the left field. "What the hell do you do on a Saturday night?"

"What the hell do you do?" Ed came back. "What woman would put up with you?"

"Oh, I got women all right. They just don't hang around very long."

Ed reflected on their condition. "You know, if you make it very far in this business, you're surrounded by more and more people, but you have less and less connection with anyone."

"You're depressing the hell out of me, Ed."

"I'm depressing the hell out of me," Ed replied.

Ed's cell buzzed. It puzzled him. A call at this late hour? He picked it up. "Yeah," he answered.

"Ed, it's Mary Barton. I hope I'm not bothering you?"

"God no, of course not, Mary," Ed's heart speeded up a bit. "What is it?"

"I've been thinking about that name you gave me, Antonio Bizzaro. I remembered where I had seen it. It was on an unsolicited movie script sent to us a few years back. I had left it on Arvin's desk, but he handed it back to me later and said, 'Chuck it.' He doesn't accept amateur scripts. But I forgot and left it in the files. It was still there."

"Very good, Mary! Do you have it? Can you send it to me?"

"Yes, we're on overtime here since Arvin's leaving soon. I'll scan it and send you a PDF copy."

"That's the second miracle for our side!" Ed exclaimed after he hung up. "First, we found Willy. Now we have Antonio!"

Mary's PDF soon showed up in Ed's mailbox. He quickly hit the print button and ran off two copies on his inkjet. He passed a copy to Bill. They sat down and started reading.

"It's a true-life mystery story," Bill revealed as he scanned through the pages.

"Yes," Ed noted. "It looks like he's written a script about being hired on a secret assignment for Howard Hughes; he's titled it *The Hughes Love Passage*."

The two men scanned the pages, looking for a storyline pertaining to a love passage.

"Listen to this!" Bill exclaimed. "He's talking about how he worked with Hughes's personal butler, Margolis on this job. Okay, here on page 46. He mentions a possible clue."

Bill read it out, "*There could be but one way to enter through the portal. There is a season, turn, turn, turn. All will be revealed.*"

"Yeah, that's it," Ed agreed. "That line has to be the code for the entrance."

Ed sat back in his chair and gathered his thoughts. "It's clear now Blackstone formulated his murder plans from this script. It was written out for him. All he had to do was play his role."

"Uh-oh!" Bill interjected. "There's a page missing. It's been removed."

"Shit!" Ed grimaced. "Blackstone must have kept the key page. But thank God Mary didn't throw the rest away. We'll just have to proceed with what we've got."

Sunday morning, Ed had had little sleep. He was up by 6 am and already at The Sylvia Hotel a good hour before he thought Sidhu would be there. But Sidhu soon arrived with his scanner case. He spotted Ed in the restaurant and sat down. "Okay, Ed," he said. "I'm ready. Tell me about this supposed pre-existing passage. What do you know?"

Ed set down his cup and rose from the table. "I'll tell you on the way up, Sidhu. Let's do it."

With the passkey from Darin, Ed opened the door and

they entered the room. There were still pieces of tape and other trash lying around. The room hadn't been touched since the night of the murder. They walked around the suite, looking for a small closet.

"That could be it," Ed nodded towards a closet door in the corner of the far bedroom.

"Let's have a look," Sidhu replied.

He opened the closet door and knelt. The floor inside had no carpet. He ran his fingers over the seams. "This is solid flooring attached to the wall," he observed. "If the floor goes down, the closet wall must go down with it. Yes, this configuration could escape my x-ray scans."

Sidhu eyed the round, decorated knobs attached to both sides of the door. "You showed me a movie script this guy wrote. In it, he mentions some code words."

Ed turned to the page. "He refers to a passage in the Bible and the lyrics of a Peter, Paul and Mary folk song back in the fifties, *There is a season, turn, turn, turn.*"

"What if we take that literally?" Sidhu suggested. "No religious or pop-folk stuff, but exactly what it says."

Ed looked at the round doorknob. "Well, what if we could we turn that?"

"Okay," Sidhu agreed. "And what's that number from the receipt again?"

Ed read it out, "*12 24 05*. But that doesn't fit as a date; this was back in 1962."

"But let's assume it's a date anyway, Ed. Not a code, but an actual date. What could it mean?"

"Well, for one thing," Ed thought, "if it's a date, then it's Christmas Eve. That could explain the word season!"

"Very good, Ed. What important Christmas date from the past could that possibly be?"

"I'm voice-checking now!" Ed brought up his cell and

spoke into it. "GOOGLE. What happened on the date 12, 24, 1905?"

"That is the birthday of Howard Hughes," came the female computer voice!

The two men stood there in astonished silence, staring at Ed's cell. Then they burst out laughing. "When in doubt, just ask!" Ed proclaimed.

"All right, Ed, we have the word 'turn' mentioned three times. Let's examine those knobs."

Sidhu studied the decoration around the outside knob. There seemed nothing unusual, but on the inside knob, he noticed some faint markings positioned around in a circle.

"I think these dots represent a clock face," Sidhu observed. "I'll try using the dates as time settings and turn the knob to those positions."

He began turning the knob, stopping on 12, then back around, stopping twice on 12 (representing 24), then back to 5. Nothing.

"Maybe the door has to be closed when you enter the numbers," Ed suggested.

"Okay, let's try that." Sidhu stepped inside the closet, turned on the light switch, and shut the door. He began turning the knob, repeating the same sequence until he stopped dead center on 5.

A discernible click!

Suddenly the floor started descending! A slight rumbling noise began. He was going down! There was no way to stop the contrivance. It continued falling, then touched the bottom.

The door popped open!

A startled man and woman jolted upright in their bed. The poor woman began screaming, the man clutching her in frozen fear!

Sidhu stood poised like a man standing in an upright

casket. He raised his arms as if surrendering. "I'm sorry! I'm so sorry!" he pleaded. "Please forgive me. I'm leaving now; I'm with the Police. I mean you no harm."

"Get out! Get out!" The man began shouting over the poor woman's screaming. Sidhu bolted towards the door. It was locked. He struggled to unlatch it. "I'm sorry!" he kept repeating as he fumbled with the lock. Finally, it opened. He turned, made a deep bow to the couple, and quickly left.

Hotel Manager Darin arrived just in time to see Sidhu ushered into the security office. "Bruce, what's this about?" he asked.

"I don't know, boss. Sidhu has gone ape. He went down to the 7th floor and broke into a couple's room, scaring them to death. They set off the fire alarm. The fire trucks were coming."

The shaken Sidhu looked at Darin. "I'll explain later. You best go up to 802 now."

Ed was standing by the door at 802 when Darin arrived up to the 8th floor. "I think we've breached your security system," Ed confessed as they entered.

Darin walked over and gazed down the gaping hole in the closet. "Good God, Ed, how did you guys do that?"

"It's been here for over 60 years," Ed replied. "It's a small secret elevator, electrically driven on a gear track hidden in the inner surface. Its walls are thin veneer and slide along the rear wall. We're the second guys to use it since then. The killer was the first."

Bill and Andy had been scanning videos all morning. They were almost out of hope when Ed's excited call came. "Bill, it's not room 702," Ed revealed. "We found the passage. It goes down to room 703 instead."

"How did you find it?"

"We found it the hard way, Bill. It seems Hughes preferred

51

going down to see his women instead of having them come up to him. Guess he didn't want anybody visiting his private lair. I'm going down there now."

Ed and Sidhu entered room 703. The frightened couple had by now been relocated, and had left the room as it was. The two men went over to the open closet.

"The old shaft came through this room instead," Ed noted. "That's why Blackstone rented both. He wasn't taking any chances."

"Yes, and notice the door is still open," Sidhu exclaimed. "If anyone had shut it, it would have tripped the switch and sent the device back up to 802."

Ed was puzzled. "If Blackstone came here later, how did he get it to come down for him?"

"There can be only one explanation," Sidhu reasoned. "Since Blackstone had managed the reservations for these two rooms himself, he had access to them plus the RK's room on the 8th floor. So he secretly entered 802 earlier that day, with his pass key, and rode the device down, and left it open. Then, around 11:30 p.m, when RK was up in 802, he came back here, stepped inside the device, and took it back up. RK wouldn't hear it coming—it's in the far bedroom. Blackstone stepped out, surprised RK, and did the deed. Then he came back down, stepped out, shut the door, and the elevator automatically returned to 802. A perfect crime."

It was precisely 11:24 on the video readout when Bill and Andy first spotted No Nose coming off the elevator. Bill had been watching zombie look-a-likes for so long now that he had given them nicknames.

No Nose went straight to room 703, pulled out his key, and entered.

"He looks about the right height," Andy noted, "and the

time matches. That's our killer, for sure. Let's see when he comes out."

Andy scanned ahead—703's door soon opened. No Nose appeared; he went straight to the elevator. The time was 11:47 p.m.

"The bastard just killed RK," Bill declared. "Don't lose him!"

Andy quickly switched to the ground floor exits on the split-screen. They waited.

"There he is," Bill pointed to a figure leaving by an exit in the main lobby. "He's leaving through the rear exit and walking toward the east parking lot."

Andy zoomed in, trying to follow No Nose. "Damn, he's walking out of range."

Bill was getting frustrated. "Do we have any parking lot footage?"

"Not from this building," Andy noted. "He's on the Tower cameras now."

"How about getting the Tower videos?"

"We can try, but they may have been deleted by now."

Bill leaned back in his chair. "Dammit, Andy, I had the RCMP ready to go into that complex and haul Blackstone's ass out. But if we can't ID him, we can't stop him from leaving tomorrow."

Darin Lawson got Bill's call. He immediately assigned Bruce to retrieve the Tower security videos, but when Bruce called back, it was bad news.

"They've dumped those videos, Boss," he reported. "Nothing here now."

"Alright, Bruce, thanks. I'll tell Bill."

On his walk back from the tower, Bruce began reasoning where Blackstone could have possibly gone after leaving the hotel property. Bruce knew this area well. All the parking around the Sylvia was residents-only, and so was the Tower. Plus, that was the festival night. There wouldn't have been any parking anywhere. So where did he park? Then it occurred to Bruce, Easy Park was over on Barclay, five blocks away. Blackstone could certainly have walked that.

The man on duty at Easy Park was accommodating as soon as Bruce introduced himself as Security from The Sylvia. "I'm interested in any security footage you might have a week back," he inquired.

"Saturday night, a week ago?" Manager Jimmy Allen replied. "Sorry, no security videos. But maybe you won't need them. What's the guy's plate number?"

"All I have is his name, Arvin Blackstone, with UnDead Studios. It would have been around 11:00 p.m. last Saturday."

"Man, I remember that name. Yeah! Big car. The guy came in with a business suit on, but when he came back later, he was wearing ragged clothes. He had red paint smeared on him. Oh yeah! For sure, I remember that guy."

Bruce could feel his heart start to race. "Do you have a copy of his ticket?"

"Got it on the computer. He paid cash, but I still keep records. I can pull it up." In a few seconds, Jimmy's screen stopped on a list of numbers.

"There's his plates and his car, a 2018 BMW, registered to UnDead Studios."

Bruce tried to control his excitement. "Jimmy, hang on, okay! I'm going to make a call to Inspector Ed Steelside. Man, there are many people who wanna talk to you."

Ed was just getting ready to get in his car to meet with Bill when his cell buzzed. It was Loren on the line. He hesitated—he needed no more negative crap. But he answered.

"Yes, Loren."

"I've heard from Sidhu. I know what's going down now. I've released Cal. I want to give you my apologies. I was wrong; we all were wrong. I want to continue working with you. Are we good?"

"Shouldn't be any problem, Loren. Of course, we're good." Ed's call alert buzzed. It showed an urgent message from Bruce. "Hold on, Loren. I'll get right back."

"Yes, Bruce." Loren could hear Ed talking loudly on the other line. "What? Holy shit! Really? Where? Stay right there! Okay! I'll be there in 15. Excellent work!"

He switched back to Loren. "We've got him, Loren! We've found an eyewitness. We've nailed Blackstone's ass!"

Bill and Ed arrived at the Easy Park at about the same time. Ed began taking down statements from Jimmy Davis while Bill contacted Maple Ridge RCMP. He clicked off his cell; he couldn't believe their bad timing.

"Damn it, Ed," Bill said. "The RCMP just informed me Blackstone's left the complex. The guard out there didn't know where he was going. I don't want to call his office. That might tip him off. What do we do now?"

"Okay, hang on." Ed picked up his cell and tapped on Mary Barton's number. She answered. "Mary, are you still at work?"

"Oh, hello Ed, just leaving. Is there anything the matter?"

"We sent some people out to a... visit Arvin at your studio, but he left earlier. Has he changed his Monday morning flight? Is he leaving now?"

"Oh no, that's still on. He's gone to Langley for a sneak preview of the new movie at the Colossus Cineplex Theater."

Ed and Bill were now driving back to their station. "We can make it out there in about an hour," Bill suggested. "Meanwhile, Langley police can hold him for us."

"I've got an even better idea, Bill; there are some people who owe us right now." Ed picked up his cell. He hit Chief Bower's tab; the Chief was in.

"Chief, it's Ed Steelside. I just wanted to fill you in."

"Good work, Ed. I just heard from Loren. Are you ready to make an arrest?"

"That's why I'm calling. Can you get me a helicopter? I'd like to pick up Blackstone myself. He's out in Langley right now; we could have the Langley RCMP arrest him. But it will look much better if the Vancouver PD nailed his ass."

"I like that, Ed. I can have our police chopper available for you from the downtown Burrard Inlet heli-pad. We'll hold it for you until you get there."

Arvin Blackstone had just arrived to meet with his promotion manager in the big theater screening area. Inside the auditorium, hundreds of fans would soon gather for the new feature film debut of *Zombies on a Plane*.

"I want all the news affiliates here," Blackstone pressed his PR guy. "Every station, you got that? When I come out for the presentation for the top producer award of the year, I want coverage upfront—my face, my name. Okay? What local politicos have you rounded up for me?"

"We've got the premier—donated a ton to his campaign. Also, the Vancouver mayor is coming. He's going to deliver a speech about how much business your film is generating—the usual boilerplate of PR."

"Fine, I want to roll with this precisely at 7 o'clock. Now get on with it!"

The big police chopper was sitting ready at the Burrard heli-pad when Ed and Bill arrived. They hurried towards the waiting aircraft. "Bill, you know the plan," Ed reminded him. "You take care of this end. Hopefully, everyone we notified is on the way here."

"I've talked to Loren and Anita Fielding, she hasn't left for LA yet, I've arranged for a police car to escort them both."

"Good," he replied, "I'll be back!" They both laughed at Ed's accidental Terminator quip.

A uniformed officer was waiting near the perimeter. Ed joined him, and the two men ducked their heads and scurried under the swirling blades. The rotors washed violently, flapping the men's light summer clothes. Ed put on the headphones and spoke to the pilot over the roaring noise.

"We got a stop in Burnaby for a pickup, then the Langley Colossus Cineplex. I've cordoned off a spot there on the parking lot for you."

The sun was low across the Pacific horizon, painting the landscape with orange and yellow hues as the chopper climbed high. They turned southward down the valley, passing over No.1 Hwy., an endless metal river glittering in the afternoon light. A clutch of townhouses soon appeared below. Ed pointed to a parking lot where several cars were parked in a circle. A police officer was waving. The chopper landed, and another man boarded the aircraft. As they lifted off, Ed turned and smiled at the man.

"Glad you could make it, Cal."

Looming ahead through the chopper's dome, Ed could make out the eastern township of Langley. Ed eyed the pilot again. "Stay with the chopper after we land. We won't be long."

The big theater was packed full of enthusiastic, shouting zombie fans. Blackstone was seated upfront. He rose from his seat, went to the podium, and stood waving at the crowd, soaking in their admiration.

"I want to tell you," he began, his voice amplified over the din, "what a pleasure I've had creating, and directing this new outstanding feature film. I guided it; it's our best movie yet, and I'm…"

Suddenly a figure barged in and grabbed the mike away from Blackstone. A police officer came forward and wrestled Blackstone away. Cal Morrow now appeared with the mike.

"Zombie fans," Cal announced to the stunned audience, "that man there," he pointed to the now restrained Blackstone, "had nothing to do with this movie. I know because I wrote this movie. My name is Cal Morrow, and this man stole my movie from me. But he is worse than a liar and a thief. He murdered my mentor, R.K. Fielding, one of the great moviemakers we all admired. Arvin Blackstone took this man from us. May he rot in Hell for his cowardly crime."

The yelling and boos against Blackstone were deafening as the policeman led him off stage. Cal remained and gave them the speech they should have been given. In the front row, Mary Barton was both smiling and sobbing at the same time.

Blackstone was handcuffed, and taken over to the waiting chopper. They placed him in the back with the Vancouver police officer, then it lifted off and disappeared into the northwestern horizon.

A small crowd stood waiting, watching the sky for the police chopper's arrival. Soon all eyes caught sight of the approaching helicopter, glistening with bright red and yellow stripes as it settled down onto its pad at Burrard Inlet. The pilot shut off the engine, the whirling blades slowed, then finally stopped.

Three men got off the aircraft, and began walking towards the assembled crowd. All around the perimeter, press cameras from every news source recorded the event.

Bill Doland walked up and joined Ed. They shook hands, and then together, the two detectives led the handcuffed

Blackstone along the line of assembled spectators.

When they approached Anita Fielding and Loren Masters, Ed slowed down their pace noticeably. Blackstone did not look up as Anita watched him pass. They continued on to a waiting police van. Blackstone ducked his head, entered the van, and they drove off.

Anita smiled. The sun definitely shone much brighter for her now.

"It was a spectacle right out of a Hollywood thriller, when hard-nosed detective Edwin Steelside swooped down on a Langley theater, and plucked out movie mogul Arvin Blackstone. It is now revealed that Blackstone was the evil mastermind behind the murder of his ex-boss, R.K. Fielding. The brutal killing involved a Howard Hughes secret love passage created by a genius carpenter at the historic Sylvia Hotel.

After his false detainment, Cal Morrow, now CEO of UnDead Studios, announced a legal probe into fraud and kickbacks by former CEO Blackstone.

Detective Steelside cited many who helped him solve this crime, especially a long-time retired employee of The Sylvia Hotel, Willy McTavish. Willy will be given a full banquet in his honor at that hotel.

Brenda Starling reporting…Watch for the complete CBC documentary, The Secret of the Undead Room, airing tonight."

URI'S FULL-BODIED WINE

"Uri Alecia Bablonski!" came a loud yell. "I know you are in here. Answer me now, Uri, or there will be hell to pay."

"Go away, Honrich Golonovich! I have no time for you." The echoing reply resounded from somewhere deep within the building's interior.

"You cannot hide from me forever, Uri. We talk now, damn you."

Banging footsteps soon indicated the caller had found the steel stairs leading up to the big open fermentation tank.

"What do you want, Honrich? I am working now. You cannot get paid if I do not work."

The heavyset man reached the top of the stairs. He paused to grab the railing and catch his breath.

"Paid? What have you paid? I have not seen one dime from you."

Uri set down the big metal wrench he was holding and took up a rag to wipe his greasy hands.

"See this piping system, Honrich," he said to the man, "it took weeks to install, and I still need to tune all the gauges. Making wine takes time."

Honrich came forward on the catwalk, pointing angrily to the giant vat. "The wine still sits in the tank. Nothing has changed since I last saw you." He took out his cell, waving it in Uri's face. "Six times, I call you, and you do not answer. We need to have wine bottled, ready to ship, and ready to SELL."

Uri batted away the phone. "I'm out in those fields, sweating in the scorching sun, minding the grapes, working myself to death, and that's all you have contributed, calls?"

Honrich shook his finger in Uri's face. "You have accomplished nothing. You fall behind the payments to me. We agreed on a schedule."

"The weather sets the schedule, Honrich. You know from nothing of grape growing."

"I see your sales figures. They are sales failures. I see three big tanks here, and you still do not bottle. Now I see you are even further behind. You are losing me money."

"You see nothing, Honrich Golonovich! I spit in your face. You are nothing but a hindrance to me. You get no money today. Leave my winery now, or I throw you out like I throw out the slag that rots in the runoffs!"

"Oh, you think so?" Honrich's voice was loud and mocking. "Have you checked the agreement you signed?" He reached into his coat pocket and waved the contract in Uri's face. "I own fifty-one percent! I'm selling this winery and deducting all the expenses you owe me. You will have nothing when I get through with you," he roared. "NOTHING!"

Honrich turned and headed for the stairs.

"YOU WOULD SELL ME OUT?" Uri screamed in a rage. He grabbed the steel wrench and swung it as hard as he could.

Honrich turned, but it was too late–the heavy wrench struck him square in his chest. He staggered backward, tumbled over the railing, and fell headlong into the huge vat.

Uri dropped the wrench in shock as Honrich's body disappeared into the swirling liquid. He staggered and collapsed onto the grated steel platform.

"God in heaven," Uri stammered. "What have I done?"

Katerina had heard the shouting from the backyard of the house. She rushed into the wine barn.

"Uri, where are you?" She called out from the winery's floor. "What is happening? Answer me!"

"I am up here, Kat," Uri answered. "Come quick! There's been a terrible accident."

Katerina made her way up the steep stairs. She found Uri lying on the platform. She looked around—where was Honrich? "What accident?" she demanded. "What do you mean?"

Uri stood up, his face pale and gaunt. "Katerina, Honrich is down there." He pointed into the wine tank.

"Holy shit, Uri! He fell into the vat? How?"

Uri didn't answer. He slumped back down and sat on the floor, shaken, struggling for an answer.

"My God, Uri, what happened? What in hell did you do?"

Uri was trembling as he spoke. "Kat, he was going to sell the winery, take away everything we have worked for. I had to stop him! I hit him, Kat. He fell backwards into the wine tank."

Katerina reached over and grabbed the rail for support, shaking her head in disbelief.

"That's not an accident, you fool. That's murder. What were you thinking?"

"It all happened so fast; I had no control. We will lose everything now, the winery, our livelihood." He paused, raising his head, his face full of grief. "Katerina, I will go to prison."

"No," Katerina replied. "It has to be an accident. Come now, Uri; let us go to the house. We sit down, have some wine. We find a way."

The little oak table by the bay window was usually where Katerina and Uri rested after a long day working the fields. Now they had much more urgent matters.

Kat went to the wine cabinet. "I will pour you our best

today; it will calm you. We must put this behind us."

Uri slumped his long-limbed frame into a chair, his head in his hands. "How can we put this behind us? We have a body in Tank 1, the police will come when he is missed."

Kat brought the wine. "It's getting dark now, it's Sunday and all the staff is off. We can hide the evidence." Kat's voice turned calm and measured. She carefully poured two glasses. "First, we remove the body," she said straight out.

Uri took a drink then set the glass down. "How? The body is in 3,000 liters of fermenting wine."

"We hook it with a dragline and pull it out," Kat replied her face cold as ice.

Uri shook his head; the thought was scary. "But his car, how do we get rid of that?"

"We drive it to someplace far away and ditch it."

"But there will be evidence he came here. They will know."

Kat scratched her nose. Uri knew she always did this when she wasn't sure of something.

"We take that chance," she finally replied. "But think about it. What can they prove? If they come, and they ask us, we say he came by, and he left."

"The ownership of the winery," Uri reminded her, "Honrich is the half-owner. There will be legal issues. Others will come, and they will ask questions."

Kat leaned back in her chair; she picked up her glass. "Let them ask, Uri; they have nothing. And think of this, now we are sole owners. No more Honrich and his nagging questions. Drink up, Uri Bablonski. We are the sole owners of Liquid Lust Winery now."

It was after midnight when Uri parked Honrich's car on a dark city street in nearby Penticton. Kat had wiped clean the door handles, the steering wheel and the dash with alcohol.

Honrich had left his briefcase, but Uri had removed it and any other reference to the winery.

Kat had reminded Uri that they should drive the car much farther than just the distance from Oliver. This would suggest the vehicle was driven to other places after leaving the winery.

Uri wore a long coat and had a hat pulled low over his face when he exited the car. He then walked to meet Kat, parked some blocks away. They quickly left the scene.

After they returned to the winery later that night, Uri and Kat partook in another bottle of Merlot. Uri brought up the problem of removing the body again.

"If we take the body from Tank 1, where do we get rid of it?" he wondered. "Also, Andre will ask why we empty tank."

Kat didn't answer right away; she scratched her nose as before. Uri waited.

"It's an issue but not a problem," she reasoned. "We tell Andre we think the wine is too acidic and ask him to seal Tank 1. Later down the road, we bury Honrich in some far-off place in the woods."

"You're a master conspirator, my Kat," Uri blurted out mockingly. "Who's next? Me?"

"Hah, you think so, my lapooshychka," she laughed. "My little paw, my partner in danger."

Uri laughed. They drank more wine.

Andre Leshan wondered why the boss needed him out in the field. As Cellar Master, he had chores to tend to in the tank area. But Uri had insisted he check the grapes in the far section to see if they were next for picking, but why? Andre had argued that was a task for a field hand, but Uri was insistent.

After Andre left, Uri climbed the stairs on Tank 1 and walked to the rim of the big vat. Good, he thought, there was no sign there was a body in it. He then went down to the vintner area. He was looking for any trace of last night's event. But everything was okay, no blood or anything that might reveal Honrich's demise. He thought of Kat's reasoning. Outsiders may have suspicions, but there was no indication of wrongdoing.

Uri smiled. He felt better now. Without Honrich's meddling, he was the absolute boss now. This was his winery. He then took out a tank notice slip and pasted it onto the big vat.

Kat was now busy in the office, organizing their business affairs. It would be a while until any authorities came. She would have everything ready for prying eyes. Yes, they had paid Honrich little, but they had also taken little for themselves—paid bills meant survival. Katerina also knew Honrich had few family connections in Canada after coming over from the old country. That was good, the less snooping, the better. She set about preparing the ordering papers to take the three-year-old cellar barrels of Lot-2 to bottle.

The sun was growing hot; Andre wiped his brow. He was getting frustrated. The grapes were ready for picking in the north section, he'd told Uri that. He needed to get back to the tank room, which was more important.

"Ignorant Slav," Andre cursed Uri under his breath on his way back to the wine barn. How dare this Russian peasant question his knowledge? Blending Cabernets and Merlots were his specialties, an art form. Uri knows only Pinot Noir. He's a bohunk, a Slavic grape picker. Every time Uri comes to the wine building, he causes problems. He should stay out in the vines where he belongs.

Andre parked and headed for the fermentation tanks. He checked the survey meter on Tank 1 for the pH levels. The reading was low, meaning the acids were actually high. But not a problem; he would stir the *must* formed by the fermenting grapes and then add more calcium carbonate. Also, he should check to inoculate for malolactic fermentation to reduce the acid.

Next, he started for the stairs; that's when he spotted the Action Notice sheet taped on the steel tank. He read Uri's directive:

Andre, seal this tank and set the wine aside. It is spoiled.

Andre was dumbfounded. The wine was only high in acid, not gone bad. It could be brought to level. This was outrageous! This full tank represented acres of picked grapes and months of work. It would be insane to dump it.

Andre tore the notice up and threw it in the trash.

Now a week had gone by since the incident. During that time there had been no calls or any questions regarding Honrich's whereabouts. But every time a car that looked official came up their road, Kat's heart would race with dread. Still, all was safe so far.

Kat's primary concern, though, was over-seeing the cellar. They had many aging barrels ready. It was important they now get them bottled and out to market. She called her distributor, Ann Smith, but Ann did not have good news.

"Kat," Ann began, "your wine is not well known yet. The retailers are not clamoring for your brand."

"This is not acceptable," Kat replied. "Cabernet is popular now. Why the problem?"

Ann tried to frame her words carefully. "Your wines were too early last year. Look, I know you just started up, but you need a good aged brand on the shelf."

"Ann, our next wine, Lot-2, is older. I know it will sell."

Ann hesitated a bit. "Okay, we'll try 100 cases; see how that lot goes."

Uri was out in the vineyards, hauling a load of grapes up

for crushing. His cell rang. He stopped the tractor and quieted the engine.

"Yes, Kat?"

"Uri, our first batch isn't selling well. Those three-year-old kegs in the cellar, Lot-2, are they ready? Do you think they are better?"

"Oh yes, much better. We had bottled the first year too early because we were cash short. But this is good wine."

"Okay, that is good news." Kat clicked off her cell.

"That god damn Honrich," Uri cursed, spitting out the dead man's name. It was Honrich who had forced him to bottle early. "It is good he is gone." He spat again.

The purple mass of crushed grapes in Tank 2 needed tending. Andre reached for the long-handled stir stick and began punching down the crust over the mixture. Then Uri's loud voice resounded throughout the wine building.

"Andre Leshan. Come down here!"

"Damn, what now?" Andre muttered. He dropped the stick and clambered down the catwalk stair to the winery floor.

"What is it now, Uri? I'm busy on the other tank."

Angered, Uri pointed to the green light on Tank 1.

"This tank is still active. Did you not see my directive? I want this tank shut down!"

"Listen, Uri, I have good news," Andre told him. "This wine is good." He produced the readout paper from his pocket. "Look, the pH levels are normal."

Uri's anger was growing. "I don't care about the readout; I think this wine has gone bad. It's cat's pee. I want it shut down now."

"But I'm ready to clarify this wine and fine it," Andre explained to him. "Soon, it will be ready to go to barrel." Andre held up a sample he'd drawn in a small glass. "Look," he told him. He swirled the sample, sniffed it and then sipped it. "It's smooth." He held it up to Uri. "Taste it."

Uri's face grew pale. "NO!" he yelled, recoiling back. "Get it away!" He ran from the building.

Andre stood there dumbfounded—what in the hell had just happened?

The sound of the screen door banging against the wall startled Kat. Uri barged in, running to the bathroom. Next, she could hear him gagging behind the closed door.

"Uri, are you okay?" He didn't answer. She decided to sit and wait.

Finally, Uri emerged, his face drained of color.

"I want Andre fired!" he blurted out. He sat at the table and said no more.

Kat hovered over him. "Now, what have you done?" She was in no mood for any more trouble.

"Andre disobeyed me," Uri answered. "He didn't turn off Tank1. He wants to keep its wine."

Kat sat down. "Oh God, what did you say to him?"

"I told him to do as I asked, but he argued that the wine was good. Kat, he… he drank from the tank. It was too much. I ran."

"Alright, now stop this panicking. It's not a big deal. I'll go and talk to Andre; no more talk of firing. Dammit, we need him."

She got up and left.

Kat found Andre sitting in the tank room. She put a smile on her face and approached him.

"Are you alright, Andre?"

"No," he answered. "What's wrong with that man? He's driving me crazy!"

Kat sat down next to him on the bench. "Uri is under pressure, Andre. This growing season is especially tough on him.

Could you bear with me for just a while?" she pleaded.

Andre rolled his eyes. "He gets in my way on every-thing, and lately, he's gotten worse. I can't work with that man anymore."

"I will talk to Uri; I need you to stay." Kat tried to be as convincing as she could. "Andre, you're in charge of the cellar production. If you say a wine is good, then we keep it. You have so much experience and knowledge. I'll remind Uri of that. I promise you this time it will work. Are we agreed?"

Andre nodded. Kat had fixed things as usual, but this time her promise had better hold. "Okay, just keep him away from the tanks. I can save the wine, Kat, but I need control."

"You have it."

Kat left. Hopefully, she had patched things up. But she knew she had only put out one fire and started up another. They would have to keep Tank 1 for now.

It took a good two weeks before Katerina was confronted with a dreaded inquiry on Honrich. But it didn't come up the road; it was a phone call. Her cell said it was from Toronto. She answered.

"Hello, Katerina." An older woman's voice was on the line. "I'm Ilsa Golonovich, Honrich's sister. I don't know if he ever mentioned my name to you?"

Tension swelled up in Kat's throat. "Yes, he's mentioned you, but I don't believe we've met."

"Oh, no, that's not why I'm calling. I can't seem to locate Honrich. He was coming to visit, but he never showed up. I called his home number and office, but no one there has seen him either."

Kat paused, then asked, "When was he to visit you, Ilsa?"

"Well, he was supposed to arrive a few days ago. Do you know anything? Has he been out to see you?"

Kat hesitated again. This was the big question. "Um, ah, let's see,... he was out here two weeks ago on Sunday, but we've heard nothing from him since."

"Well, okay then, Katerina, thank you. But if you do hear anything, please call me at this number. We are anxious here, and it's not like him just to disappear."

"Of course, Ilsa. Sorry I couldn't help you."

At lunch, Kat informed Uri of the call. She broke it to him as gently as she could. "This tells us that Ilsa will file a missing person report," she began. "We need to sync up our stories; the police will soon want to talk to us."

Uri set his wine down. "Did you ask her if Honrich had said anything about us, anything about selling?"

"No," Kat came back. "That's the worst approach, Uri. Never ask questions that hint at a motive. Never give information until you've heard it from the questioner first."

"How you know all this stuff?" Uri asked suspiciously. "You talk like master felon!"

"It's common sense; just remember it."

"All I know, Kat, is we must get body from the tank soon. Police will be here; they will search with special equipment. They will find evidence."

"Yes, I've thought of that," Kat assured him, "and I have a plan."

"You have a plan? I have a plan too. We tell Andre we are boss, we empty tank. He stays out of it." Uri sat back, his arms folded.

"Listen, Uri," Kat knew this was going to be rough. "We need Andre on our side. Let him barrel the tank as this year's Lot-3. When the tank is near empty, we send Andre away on a mission or something. Then we can dispose of evidence, and all is good."

Uri said nothing. Kat could see his face redden. He brought his fist down hard on the table, rattling the cabinet dishes.

"NO!" he bellowed. "I do not want that wine barrelled. It is poison. It keeps Honrich's ghost alive. He will haunt me from the cellar. We must destroy all trace of him."

Kat sat back; she crossed her arms, her eyes fixated on Uri. The only sound, the old clock ticking in the hallway.

"Did you hear what you just said, Uri Bablonski?" Her voice was accusing. "Do you want to go to prison because you believe in ghosts? Are you ready to send me there too?"

Uri shook his head. "Andre is only an employee. He must do what we tell him."

"He is Cellar Master, Uri. He believes that wine is good, and he will make trouble. When the police come, anything unusual will focus their suspicion on that tank. Do you want that?"

Uri calmed a bit. "No, but there must be another way. This is too scary for me."

"After the wine is drained and filtered, it will sit for three years in barrels," Kat replied. "We will have all that time to get rid of it. Plus, we still have the other two tanks. It will not be so big a loss. We can survive."

"I must have time to think, Katerina. I do not like this."

"Nor do I, Uri, but we must stay calm and focus. Do you agree or not?"

Uri nodded, but Kat could see he wasn't convinced.

Andre entered the tank room, and pulled the plastic hose from Tank 1, it ran a cloudy red. But that was good. Andre knew the filters would solve it. Wine is always cloudy at the early pull. He shut off the drain spigot when the smaller settling tank topped off. He capped it and smiled. It was done. This full settling tank signified Lot-3, the cellar's first wine of

71

the year. In another week, he would have the entire batch from Tank 1 ready to barrel.

That night Kat informed Uri of Andre's near completion of the draining of Tank 1.

"We need to remove the body from that tank now, Uri. Andre will drain down to where it is soon."

She studied Uri's nervous reaction; the removal of the body was causing an issue with him.

"Uri, we're running out of time," Kat reminded him. "We discussed this. The long weekend is coming; it will be perfect. Most of the staff will be gone, except for Andre and Gwynn Williams, the storeroom worker."

Uri nervously nodded. "Okay, we ask Gwynn to leave early, but how do we get Andre away from the tanks? He's always in the fermentation room."

"There's a wine seminar in Kelowna this weekend," Kat noted. "I'll ask him to represent us at the meetings. He'll like that. All the other Cellar Masters will be there."

"I need time to think."

"Uri, I need your commitment to this. I can't do it by myself. You must drop this fear you have."

"Kat, I am bothered by that tank; I'm afraid to go near it! Honrich is in that tank; he will be in those bottles." Uri was obsessed. "I had nightmares last night. He hovers like death over me from that tank."

"Okay. Okay. I believe you, Uri." She sat in thought for a moment. "Maybe I have something that can help you."

Kat arose and went to her desk drawer. She opened it and brought out a small wooden box. "Take this, Uri," she said, handing it to him.

The box was latched with a little catch. Uri snapped it open. Inside was a silver object; he took it out and examined it.

"It's a Domovoy," Kat informed him. "My babushka gave it to me when I was a little girl in the old country."

Uri studied the little elfish figure dangling from a leather strap. A long curving mustache framed his fierce-looking face. A pointed hat sat on his head, surrounded by symbols of stars. "Yes, I've seen this in old country," Uri smiled. "My mother also had one."

"It's a Chechen talisman, Uri. The Domovoy is the deity that protects our household. With it, you are safe from demon spirits. It will drive them all away."

Uri nodded his head in approval. He held the talisman in his hand. "Thank you, Katerina Bablonski." His face now brightening up. "This is good."

"Okay, Saturday morning, is it then?" Kat told him. "We do it. Yes?" She searched his face for an answer.

Uri placed the talisman strap around his neck. "Yes, my Kat, we do it."

Kat smiled. She had bought the little figure on eBay for $24.95. Better a lie that heals, she thought, than a truth that harms. It was an old Russian proverb.

Kat and Uri walked to the wine barn, the air turning colder. Kat looked to the darkening sky, hinting at a threat of rain. Uri had suggested they bury the body on the western mountain slope. It was dense with thick brush, rarely visited. But she didn't like the possibility of trudging in mud, packing a wine-soaked corpse.

Uri went up to the big tank and peered inside. The tank was still one-quarter full, but it mainly was pulp now. Fortunately, the body was still unexposed. A few more days of draining, and Andre would have seen it.

This was terrifying to Uri, he looked away from the tank. He would have to prepare himself now to enter the vat. He took hold of the grappling hook attached to the crane hoist on a rail above the tanks. It would make the lifting easier. He was wearing a clumsy rubber bodysuit and a breathing mask used for tank cleaning. He transferred his weight to the hook, and Kat pushed the hoist button to lower him down into the red mulch.

Once down, Uri fished around in the muck with his hands until he found the sunken remains. He positioned himself and wrapped a rope around the body until he could fasten the hook.

"Lift!" Uri yelled. Kat hit the button.

Up from the vat came a gruesome, shriveled purple mass, bringing an overpowering stench of escaping gasses with it. The corpse rose until it was swinging high above the tank, dripping down wine and falling waste, a scene right out of a B grade horror movie.

When the body had drained off, Kat lowered it down over a heavy tarp laid on the floor. They wrapped it up and loaded it into the back of the truck. Kat locked off the tank room door, and they left.

Luckily there was no rain yet, and the road up the mountain was dry. Uri knew this area; he had driven this old, abandoned dirt road before.

Uri found the cut-off he remembered and edged the 4-wheel drive truck into the brush. The rest of the way would be by carrying. Kat wasn't a big woman, but she was stronger than most, and somehow they transported the body to their hidden digging site.

They began digging. Hours went by until Uri felt the hole was deep enough. They rolled in the body and emptied two bags of lye over it. The lye would kill any smell that might attract animals, plus help to dissolve the corpse. The final step was to fill in the hole again, so all evidence was buried.

As darkness fell, a silent full moon lit the valley, revealing deep shadows in ghostly detail along the winding road down.

Uri drove with one hand on the wheel, holding the talisman tight in the other. He felt better. At last, the deed was done. The ghost was gone.

Even at five in the morning, the summer sun in the South Okanagan Valley shines warm and bright, stealing back the night too soon. By six o'clock on most days, Uri would be out somewhere in the winery, working.

Kat always used this time to tend to her flowers behind the house. She had trellises all around the back patio, covered with climbing roses and purple morning glory. It was here she could listen to the gurgling water fountain as she tended to their cuttings. This was the perfect place to usher in the winery's visitors, a green and welcoming spot where they could sit and enjoy a tasting.

She wouldn't expect any visitors this early; most tourists and wine enthusiasts didn't arrive until later. She had this quiet time for herself.

But on the Tuesday morning after the disposal of the body, the slam of car doors startled her; she hadn't heard the car drive up. She set her trimmings down and hurried inside to the front desk. A tall man in a grey suit stood in the doorway. Another man was behind him. He looked around, saw Kat, and came forward.

"Hello," he greeted her. "I'm looking for Uri and Katerina Bablonski."

"I'm Katerina," she answered. "My husband is out in the winery now."

"Katerina, if you don't mind, we'd like to speak to you both. Please inform him to come up."

"Um, regarding?"

"Just routine questioning." He motioned to the other man. "This is officer Dean; I'm Inspector Dexter Mallory, Penticton

RCMP. We can wait outside."

"You can take a seat out on the terrace if you like," she told them, pointing to the patio. "I'll call him."

Soon Uri brought his tractor up the hill. He parked near the office, but Kat met him before he reached the house. He was obviously tense.

"Be calm; they just want to talk," she whispered. "No big deal."

The two officers greeted Uri, and then they all took a seat on the patio. Officer Mallory opened his notebook and looked at Uri. "I understand you and your wife share this property with another owner, Honrich Golonovich. Is that correct, sir?"

"Yes, he's a half-owner," Uri replied. "But he hardly ever comes around. Kat and I run the place full time."

"When did you see him last?"

"Why?" Uri blurted out.

Kat came in. "It was about four weeks ago," she said.

Mallory glared at Kat. "Let Uri answer, please."

He looked back at Uri. "What was the nature of his visit?"

Uri began stammering a bit. "I, um, well, he just came by to see us. He sometimes comes to visit, see how we're doing. Check up on things, you know."

Mallory looked over at Kat. "And at what times did he arrive and leave, Mrs. Bablonski?"

"He was here on Sunday the first of the month," she quickly replied. "Uri showed him the cellar storage. Then he left about two hours later, around six p.m."

Now Mallory stared intently at Uri. "How do you get along with Honrich? Any angry confrontations with him, any trouble that way?"

Uri put his hand to his forehead. His first reaction was to lie. He looked at Kat, but she was trying to reveal little emotion.

"I… I wish I could say we get along, Officer, but I can't."

Uri hesitated, then collected his thoughts. "Yes, we have many differences. Honrich is novice in wine growing. He makes life difficult for us. We both put up with him."

The Officer nodded. He looked to Kat. "Has anybody else contacted you asking about him?"

Kat immediately realized they'd talked to Ilsa. "Yes, his sister called about two weeks ago. She was looking for him. She couldn't seem to locate him."

"That didn't cause you any alarm?"

"Yes, of course, and I was sympathetic to her. But we have a winery at peak season."

"Okay, that will do it for now," Mallory concluded. "I just have one more request. I would like the names of your key employees. We would like to talk to them now as well."

Kat froze. This was unexpected. "Officer, they're busy in the daytime. Can't it be later?"

"I have a schedule also, Mrs. Bablonski," Mallory reminded her. "We'll try not to disrupt your people too much. Just give me the names."

"Is Honrich now an official missing person?" Katrina asked.

"Yes, he is our top priority right now."

That night, Kat and Uri were at their little table by the window. They were worried now that the police were involved. Kat poured the wine. Uri was quiet.

"Look, Uri, the cop was just fishing; he knew nothing," she consoled him. "He was just looking for reactions. You handled it very well, I thought."

"Somebody must have talked," Uri mumbled. "The cop was suspicious. He went around, he talk to our staff, taking photographs. What's he looking for?"

"He's got a missing person case, Uri. He has to question

everybody." Kat picked up her glass. "We have to patch things up with Andre, treat him good, okay?"

Uri tapped his glass on hers. "Okay, agreed."

With the added workload at this time of year, Kat decided Gwynn Williams, who had been with the winery for a year now, should be promoted and take on additional responsibilities. He had been a sommelier at a restaurant when Kat had first hired him. Then Andre had trained him well in his job as Assistant Cellar Master. Plus, his knowledge of wine marketing was a valuable asset at any winery. Now Andre assigned Gwynn to the cellar, so he would soon be responsible for bottling and barrel samplings.

The following morning an article appeared in The Penticton Herald when it arrived in the mailbox:

Co-owner of Oliver winery missing. *Police are seeking the whereabouts of Honrich Golonovich, first reported missing by his sister Ilsa Golonovich last week. Honrich was last seen in the Oliver area over a month ago at the Liquid Lust Winery. His vehicle, a 2015 Toyota sedan, was recently found abandoned on a city street in Penticton. Police suspect possible foul play. If you have any information regarding Honrich, please call Inspector Dexter Mallory at Penticton RCMP.*

This was both good news and bad for the Bablonskis. Now there were more drop-by visitors at Liquid Lust. Kat and Uri had gained some degree of notoriety in the wine valley's small circle. They had a tantalizing mystery going. A member of the local wine establishment was missing, providing intriguing tidbits of chatter. But it had also focused the attention of the police on the winery. Katerina knew they must carefully guard their daily activities.

Things proceeded well at the winery, then one dreaded day late in the growing season, that all changed.

Kat shielded her eyes from the sun. It was unusually hot, especially for late September. Below on the property, she could see Uri tending to the lower vineyard sprinklers. Just as Kat was about to turn back to the house, a black Mercedes appeared, winding its way up the slope. It wasn't a supplier, she knew all their cars, and it was too early for any customers. This could be trouble. She went back into the house.

The driver stepped from the car. He was tall, thin with a dark complexion, wearing a black leather sports jacket. He stood in the lot, looking over the property, noting the vintner building. He turned and walked towards the house.

"May I help you?" Kat greeted him, standing up from her front desk.

"Yes, I'm looking for the owner of this property." His voice and manner were friendly, but firm.

"I'm Katerina Bablonski," Kat answered. "My husband and I own this property."

"Very good then. Can I talk to you?"

"Of course." Kat motioned to her small office chair.

"Well, Katerina," he replied, taking a seat, "may I call you that?"

"Everyone calls me Kat. And you are?"

"Jorge Blackmore, I'm a business associate of Honrich Golonovich. I believe he's a co-owner of this property."

"He's a silent partner," Kat immediately came back, somewhat concerned. "What business do you have with Honrich, may I ask?"

Jorge frowned. He reached into his coat pocket and produced a folded sheet of paper.

"This is an agreement signed by Mr. Golonovich, regarding a certain loan he and I entered into." He handed the paper to Kat. "In that agreement," Jorge went on, "he placed his holdings as collateral."

Kat unfolded the paper. It was a hand written document, not exactly official looking to her.

"I've heard nothing of this," Kat replied. "Precisely what holdings are you referring to?"

Jorge raised his arm and made a sweeping motion. "This property," he gestured. "Read the document; this winery is mentioned at the bottom."

A wave of both fear and anger swept across Kat. She took a deep breath. "Just why are you here, Jorge? We accept no agreement made separately without our knowledge." Kat kept her cool. "I think you should talk to Honrich; none of this is our concern."

"Oh, but it is now, Kat. It seems my business partner, your co-owner, has disappeared." He gave Kat a little smirking smile. "So now I have only you."

Kat disregarded him. "If you're looking for some wine, I can help you. Otherwise, I have work to do. Please leave."

Jorge leaned in close, his voice now menacing. "You won't get rid of me that easy, Katerina." He laid a card on the table. "Call me soon, or maybe I will have a little chat with your new friend Mallory. We both know I won't find Honrich. Don't we, Katerina?"

He turned then and left.

A pang of sheer terror tingled down Kat's spine as she watched the Mercedes drive away.

At the table that night, Kat poured Uri a glass of the good stock. She sat silently as he sipped. Then she mentioned Blackmore and showed him his card.

Uri's face reddened. "Who is this sorry bastard? He has no claim on us!"

"I think he knows something the police don't," Kat replied,

setting her glass down. She framed her words carefully. "He says that with Honrich nowhere to be found and therefore no way to be paid, the winery should cover his debt. He's trying to force a deal somehow!"

Uri winced. "What do we do?"

Kat held up the card. "Let's find out what he knows."

Jorge Blackstone parked his Mercedes and came to the winery office at 8:30 p.m., as Kat had requested. She ushered him into the big tank fermentation room. All the staff was gone now except for Uri, who was above on the platform stirring Tank 2.

Kat motioned to Jorge to take the steel stairs up. Jorge didn't like this; he was in an alien environment. But he climbed and then made his way along the platform.

Uri was stirring the wine pulp. Pungent fumes were spewing out. He noticed Jorge approaching; he took out the stick and set it aside.

"Okay, I give you a meeting," Uri said to the man, taking off his gloves. "Tell me now what you want?"

"It seems your partner owes me a great deal of money," Jorge answered. "I think we can come to some agreement on settling that debt."

"No, I doubt that. Why should we settle any of his bad business with you?"

"One reason," Jorge said. "To keep my knowledge of this whole affair confidential."

Uri's face reddened. "What affair?"

"Your little visit with Honrich—the police will be very interested in that."

"You know nothing of our meeting with Honrich." Kat quickly came in. "How could you? You weren't even here!"

Jorge's eyes tightened. "He came up here to see you Sunday

night, August 1, at precisely 8:17 p.m."

Kat recoiled in shock. She had not revealed that time to anybody. "How do you know that?"

"Because I was waiting for him down at that god damn pub after he dropped me off. But he never came back. He never left this winery. Did he?"

Kat tried to speak, her voice cracking. "He left. He went home!"

"No, he didn't! He came here to get money from you, to pay me. That's why I was with him. I waited for three hours in that damn pub. But he never returned." Jorge's voice turned calm and measured. "You killed him, didn't you?"

"He's not dead. He's a missing person," Uri stammered.

"Oh, he's dead alright. The cops suspect foul play now."

"Then, if you believe that," Kat challenged him. "Why haven't you gone to the police?"

"At first I figured he'd flown the coop," Jorge came back, "but when they found his ditched car, I knew then you bastards had done him in."

"What do you want?" Kat asked coldly.

"He owed me $150,000."

"Bullshit, you're lying. Besides, we won't pay that."

"Oh yes, you will, plus $25,000 interest. You'll be taking over his instalments. I'm your new silent partner," he sneered.

"You bastard thief!" Uri shouted. He came forward menacingly.

Blackmore yanked open his coat, revealing a holstered pistol. "Go ahead!" he shouted. "Did you think I would come unarmed?"

At that moment, Kat lunged forward, slamming hard into Jorge, knocking him back to the edge of the tank. He stood dangling over the edge, desperately flailing his arms, trying to keep from falling.

Kat hit him again. He screamed—plunged headfirst into the tank, and sank into the dark liquid, his arms reaching out, fingers grasping at thin air.

Then he was gone.

Kat looked over at a stunned Uri. "Let's get him out now. Then we need to hide the car."

THREE YEARS LATER
Representing the age of a fine Cabernet

"Look, Mommy," the little girl happily exclaimed, "Jody's found a hand."

The mother peered down to see the little dog holding a dark-looking object in its mouth. It appeared to be a human hand.

"Achhhh! Get it away!" she screeched.

Her husband came running over, examined the shriveled object, and then dropped it in disgust. "Alice, get the cell; we better call the police."

Chief Inspector Dexter Mallory was watching a softball game with his family when he got the call from dispatch.

"Yeah? Are you sure it's human? Yeah. Okay. I'll be up there in about an hour." He clicked off.

"What's that all about?" his wife asked.

"Some picnickers found a body part up in the mountains above Oliver."

"No! Where?"

"Up around Fairview Road on some old logging road."

As Mallory bounced along the rutted road leading to the site, he tried to recollect the old missing person reports. Most were derelicts or lost tourists, but there had been none from the Oliver area for some time.

Mallory pulled into a turnoff and parked by an open field. An older man was waiting.

Dr. Ellery Wilson was the local Forensic Pathologist from Penticton, an expert on body decomposition. He was always the go-to guy in these cases. He greeted Dexter and led him across the field until they reached a washed-out area leading up the mountain.

"The dog found the hand here," Ellery explained. "My guess is the rest is up there." He pointed up the steep slope.

"How did it get down here?" Dex asked. "That's a good 1000 meters up."

"There was a heavy rain here a few days ago; it washed down this ravine," Ellery replied.

Dexter took off his hat and scratched his brow. "I'll be damned. What a stroke of luck."

"That's right. If it had been buried five meters on either side of the wash, we'd never have found it."

Inspector Frederick Dean was in his office when Dexter came in Monday morning. Fred had the body part report from the lab. "Did you see this?" he asked Dex.

"Not the report yet, but I was up at the site Sunday with Ellery."

"Listen to this, the hand they found had been fermented in wine!"

"What? Gimme that." Dex took the report and read it. "Good God, Freddy! It says it had been soaked in a wine must."

"Yep, aged to perfection."

Dex groaned. "It says the rest of the body they found is in tiny pieces. Looks like only the hand is intact." He handed it back to Fred. "Go figure?"

"They mention there were traces of lye on the hand," Fred

noted. "My guess is the lye ate away most of the corpse, but the hand survived somehow. Maybe rain washed it off over time."

"Any ID yet?"

"No, but with a hand, it shouldn't take long."

Dex scratched his chin. "This is getting weirder. When I talked to Ellery, he figured the body had been there at least three years. Let's start digging out old files."

It was five p.m. when the crime lab finally called. It was Dr. Wilson.

"We got an ID match, Dex," Ellery told him. "It fits a missing person report filed three years ago for a Honrich Golonovich. A Chechen. The guy immigrated to Canada 20 years back."

"Yeah, I recognize that name—a winery owner in Oliver. He was on our rap sheet. He'd caused trouble over at the casino a couple of times."

"Also," Ellery added, "we can try to break down the wine components that soaked the hand to determine the mixture. That should help."

"That's wild, Ellery, a DNA match to ID some wine?"

Ellery laughed. "Sort of like that."

"We gotta keep this under wraps, Ellery. It'll be all over the news circuits."

"I hear you." He clicked off.

Dex turned to Freddy. "Remember that visit we made to Liquid Lust Winery a few years back? Let's do some more digging on those two."

The sun was up and Katerina was out on her garden terrace. Monday mornings were her respite, her time to relax. The new bottles were moving well, and the winery was finally making a good return. Then her cell rang; it was a caller from the

Vines Magazine.

"Hello, Katerina. It's Armando Blassa, editor with Vines magazine. I'd like to review your Cabernet Sauvignon this year. I've heard some very nice things about it."

Kat's heart jumped a beat. "Well, thank you, Armando, that's great. We just released it."

"Oh, it's very much in the mix now. The Socialistes are envious!" Armando's tone became elevated. "You must, oh, and I do mean *must*, give our writers the scoop."

"Yes, I will, Armando."

"Tremendous Katerina, we'll be in touch. Ta!"

That night Kat sat at the table, much excited. She described her call to Uri from the magazine. "This is a real coup!" She beamed. "We'll be top shelf now."

"Good," Uri responded. "Gwynn told me the first shipment almost totally sold; we'll have it all out by the end of month."

They took up their glasses and clinked. "To Liquid Lust" Kat toasted. "Un 'tres bon… whatever." She laughed. They drank.

The next day, Kat got a very positive call from Ann Smith, her distributor. "Kat, I have some good news." Ann sounded excited.

"Great, good news is welcome."

"We're not sure what's happening, but your last shipment of Lot-3 bottles is selling fast. What secret ingredient did you put in those barrels?" A terrible realization suddenly gripped Kat, Ann had said Lot-3!

"Um, I… I don't know," she stammered. "That's the first wine of that year."

"Well, send more soon, Kat. It's a hit."

Kat put her cell down and collapsed into her chair, shaking her head. "Damn," she mumbled to herself. Lot-3 was from

Tank 1; Honrich was in that wine. Lot-3 was supposed to be thrown out.

Gwynn was busy rolling barrels to storage when Kat found him in the cellar. She motioned to him, and he came over. They were standing next to the cases of wine bottles marked Lot-4.

"Gwynn, didn't I ask you to send a batch of these cases to distribution first?"

"Yes, but I thought I'd bottle Lot-3's wine and ship them instead. They're the first of that year, a little older, so I figured it might help them sell better."

"But I told you to hold them back; I was worried about them."

"Kat, I sampled Lot-3. It wasn't bad—little beefy maybe, but ready."

Kat winced. "Alright, then keep sending it."

That evening Kat sat quiet at the table. She took up a bottle and poured Uri a glass, as usual.

"Uri, I heard from Ann today. Our Lot-3 barrels—you know, they're selling better than any wine we've ever bottled."

"What? I thought you meant the magazine was all gaga over Lot-4." Uri then grasped what she implied. "Wait, Kat, I thought you threw out Lot-3 barrels!"

"Yes, but it looks like it went to market instead."

Uri looked at the bottle on the table. He grabbed it, holding it up angrily. "Kat, is this bottle from Lot-3 also?"

Kat put her hand on the bottle. "No. No! My God, Uri, the mix-up was in the shipment. God is my witness."

Uri sat back in his chair, his face now pale. "How did this happen?"

"It was Gwynn," Kat replied, shaking her head. "He informed me Lot-3 wine was good. I thought it was a miracle that batch was even drinkable. Now it's our best."

"Tell them it came from different area of field." Uri sat back, trying to think. "That's all I can say for now."

Inspector Mallory's cell buzzed; it was Dr. Wilson over at the Crime lab. Dex grabbed it up immediately.

"Dex, I've run samples of the skin fragments from the specimen, but I'm afraid there's no news on it yet."

"Can't you break down the wine mixtures?"

"No, Dex, I'm sorry. The chemical evaluation is way beyond our equipment. The hand is in too much deterioration. But there is a lab in Australia that's doing wonders in wine research called Vintessentia. I'll send it down there."

"Australia? Who would have thought?" Dex responded. "Okay then, thanks, Ellery. We'll sit tight."

Dex clicked off his cell. Damn, he was ready to storm up that hill and seal off Liquid Lust. Now he would have to sit and wait some more.

Kat and Uri greeted guests at their presentation table in the crowded hotel conference room. Kat felt comfortable, but Uri, in his ill-fitting sport coat, appeared more like a lost farmer forced into a town meeting.

They were soon introduced to Jacques Duboeuf, a well-known wine expert and writer.

"Ah, the Bablonskis," he exclaimed. "We meet at last, and you must be Katerina." He took her hand in a limp handshake. "And you, Uri, I've heard so much of your triumph."

"A, well, yes," Uri muttered somewhat taken aback, "our new lineup is good."

"Oh, you speak too modestly, Uri. Your Cabernet screams complexity."

Uri frowned, wondering what that meant.

"It hits the tongue, then leaps to the palette," Jacques went on, "leaving the senses sprinting to catch up. I detected a trace of mint, no?" He looked at Kat.

Kat cringed. Probably aftershave, she thought.

"But most of all," he declared, "there's a meaty depth— an earthy, hedonistic, bursting, muscular, throbbing taste of excitement."

He turned to Uri.

"I have a title for this new wine."

Uri tried not to wretch.

"Uri's Full-Bodied Climax," he announced, waving his hand. "That's what I will write."

Uri set down his glass and quickly sprinted for the bathroom.

"His stomach's a bit upset," Kat quickly explained. "He's been reacting badly to some sushi from lunch."

That evening Kat was driving on their way back to the Winery. Uri was tired. The constant babbling of wine talk was too much to endure. "That's the first and the last wine presentation I'm going to," he complained.

"But we met some good contacts there, Uri."

"We don't need them now. We're on a roll."

"Uri, the last of Lot-3 will be gone soon. Now, Lot-4 will have to support us."

"It will do it, Kat. Once your name is good, perception follows."

Kat was about to answer when the news came on the FM… something about Oliver….

"Turn it up, Uri!"

…"*picnickers reported the hand when their dog found it in a heavily wooded area. Police now have identified the find as part of the remains of Honrich Golonovich, a business partner of the owners of Liquid Lust Winery in Oliver. Honrich disappeared over three years ago. Police have not released any more details."*

The phones constantly rang in the winery the next morning. Kat asked Sally, her new counter helper, to field all the calls. She was too depressed to talk to anyone.

But soon Sally motioned to her, indicating an important call. Kat shook her head, no! Sally hung up and then came over. "It's from Vine Magazine. They left a number to call back."

Kat nodded to her. She got up and walked over to Uri sitting out on the patio.

"It's the writer from Vine. They want to do an article on our new wine, Uri." Thats good news."

Every since the report; Uri had been upset and had neglected the fields. Kat knew he was needed out there, but she hadn't pressed it on him.

"Uri, we will have to go on—act as if this has nothing to do with us."

"How, Kat? How they find body, it's maddening!"

"It's not that bad Uri, if there were any more evidence, they'd be here by now."

"Let's wait, Kat. We can use the time to think."

Sally was making a hand gesture—she got Kats attention, another important call. Kat took it on her cell.

"Kat here."

Ann came on the line. "Katerina, good news. Your first stocks sold out. How much do you have left over there?"

Kat cringed, thinking of the Blackmore bottles. "We have the second bottling of Lot-3. It's from that same time."

"Great send it all—oh, one other thing, have you labeled the bottles yet?"

"No. Gwynn was just going to do that."

"Listen, the ad people think you need to rebrand it—get this," Anne's voice was excited, "Uri's Full-Bodied Special

Reserve. What do you think?"

Kat shook her head, "Uh, sure. Okay Ann, have them send the labels straight over to Gwynn."

That night at the table, Kat mentioned her call from Ann. "Uri, I just released the second shipment of Lot-3."

He didn't answer. He knew what was in that shipment.

The Golonovich case was a priority again in Penticton PD. Officer Fred Dean had been scanning Honrich's phone call records. He noted one name that kept popping up in his cell calls. This name seemed familiar, Fred thought. That name was Jorge Blackmore.

This man was reported missing several weeks after Honrich's disappearance. That seemed too coincidental. But Blackmore was from Vancouver. His report didn't mention any connection with Penticton. Blackmore wasn't reported missing until he didn't pay his bills, suggesting he had few friends.

But now that Honrich's disappearance had become a homicide, Fred had asked Vancouver PD to help by checking into Blackmore's background. So when officer Bill Dolan of Vancouver PD got back to him, he was excited. He called the number Bill had left.

Bill came on the line. "We may have something here," he began. "That name Blackmore has been on my rap sheet file for years."

"That's great, Bill. What have you found?"

"This guy is a real scumbag—or was. He loaned out money he obtained from rich foreign investors who were trying to hide cash from immigration—big problem out here. He worked mostly out of the casinos; that's where he found his marks."

"How did you connect him to us?"

"We had an informant who squealed in return for less jail

time. He said he loaned Blackmore 35,000 dollars to fleece a gambler who lost big at the roulette tables."

"Wow, that's a chunk."

"Yeah. The informant told us Blackmore's pigeon was a well-heeled Slavic who owned a winery out in the Okanagan."

Fred's heart skipped a beat. "That's our guy, alright."

"I thought so too. At first, I figured Blackmore took off with the cash. But he left everything here except his car. So that told us he was probably dead."

"What kind of car was it?"

"An old black 1997 Mercedes."

After Bill hung up, Fred turned and gave a high sign to Dexter across the room. Dex smiled. At last, a good lead.

By the weekend, Gwynn had completed the last of Lot-3 and loaded the cases on a truck for delivery. He kept one box out for the tasting counter and carried it over to the office.

Kat was on the patio terrace when she saw Gwynn come in. He began unloading the bottles for display.

"No, Gwynn!" Kat announced as he removed them from the box. "Put them behind the counter."

But Gwynn held a bottle up, showing her the new label. "Look, Kat. Uri's Full-Bodied Special Reserve. Nice, huh?"

"I said, put them away!" she yelled, startling Gwynn.

"Sorry, Kat, I thought you'd be happy to see them."

Kat immediately apologized, "Forgive me, Gwynn. It's been a rough day. Just leave them."

The blinking light on Inspector Mallory's phone lit up. It was the crime lab. He grabbed it immediately. "Yes, Ellery?"

"Dex, I'm sorry. We can't positively identify a marker in the hand specimen."

"Damn," Dex replied. "What do you have? Anything?"

"The Lab Down Under tells us it has traces of Cabernet and Merlot."

The detective leaned back in his chair in frustration. "Ellery, that describes just about every red wine in the valley, hell, most of BC."

"Yeah, dead-end," Ellery replied. "The sample was exposed to the elements too long. Sorry Dex, that's about it."

Gwynn was eating lunch in the wine cellar when his cell buzzed. It was Sally at the desk.

"I got a guy from Vine Magazine on the line," Sally exclaimed, quite excited. "Kat told me to pass him on to you."

"Wow!" Gwynn was surprised. This was a big deal. "Sure, Sally, put him through."

"Hello, Gwynn, it's Kendrick Chastain, a writer with Vine. I would just love to do a story on your little Cabernet. How 'bout I visit, interview you on-site, take some pix, do the whole bio thing?"

Gwynn's heart sped up. "Of course, sure, anytime."

"Well, splendid, Gwynn, let's do it then! I'll get back to you on it soon, Ta, Ta."

Dexter Mallory and Fred Dean each pulled out a chair in the RCMP meeting room and sat at the table. Sitting across from them was District Prosecuting Attorney Mary Defoe.

Dex turned to Fred and asked him to report his findings.

"We got a break after Honrich's body was discovered," Fred began. "We could then access his finances. That told us he was deeply in debt. Since then, we've found he'd been desperate to sell his ownership of the winery, as it wasn't doing well. Also, to facilitate his growing debt, Honrich borrowed money from a loan shark out in Vancouver named Jorge Blackmore."

Fred walked to the blackboard. He chalked up Sunday, August 1, 2018, on the slate. "We're now focusing on this date.

It's when Honrich went to the winery almost exactly three years ago. That's when his two partners, Katerina and Uri Bablonski, admitted they had last seen him. He was reported missing two weeks later.

"Then a month or so after that," Fred went on, "Blackmore comes to Penticton. Why? We think he was looking for Honrich. But he goes missing also."

Mary finished writing. She removed her reading glasses. "Okay, what do you guys conclude?"

Dex crossed his arms, sitting back in his chair. "We believe Honrich met his demise the day he came out and confronted his business partners at the winery. We know there had been animosity between Uri and Honrich, there are rumors galore of their violent arguments. Maybe a fight ensued, then somehow Honrich's body, or just his hand wound up in a wine. His partners decided to hide the body. Later Blackmore shows up to put the squeeze on them. He probably met the same fate."

"That's pretty wild, Dex" Mary answered. "Can we prove that?"

"Well, we found Honrich's ditched car. The GPS had been removed, but it still tells us the crime was committed in their area, probably that same day.

"We'd like to find Blackmore," Fred added, "but we don't have his body. He's not even declared dead—just missing. We can't even prove he came out to the winery."

"You searched the winery's premises," Mary said. "Anything there at all?"

"Not much." Fred answered. There were no security cameras. The day Honrich visited was Sunday, with no staff around for witnesses. We were hoping we could've matched the wine on the victim's hand to their vineyard, but the trace was too weak. Too bad. We could have nailed their ass with that."

Dex closed his notebook. "That's where we are now. We

have a good motive, with no other suspects. What do you think Mary, do we have enough?"

The prosecutor frowned, she shook her head. "You have probable cause, lots of good circumstantial stuff here, but that's all it is. You need more evidence on Honrich's visit. It could be argued he was killed after he left the winery."

"Alright then, Dex concluded. "We'll keep looking and keep you posted."

Sally Kellerman was now on the front desk almost full time. The calls and visitor traffic were overwhelming for Kat. She spent most of her time running financial affairs, which was becoming much more demanding.

Then, Ilsa Golonovich, Honrichs sister called.

"Katerina," Ilsa came on, "so sorry I haven't got back to you sooner; I've been so busy with Honrich's death, and of course, so shocked."

"Yes, Ilsa, we are here too."

"Katerina, it seems Honrich has willed his share of the winery to me, but I know nothing of the wine business. I don't know what to do!"

Kat held her breath; this could be good. "How can I help you, Ilsa?"

"I thought maybe we could meet with the mortgage company and work out some kind of arrangement of sale if you are interested."

"Yes, of course, Ilsa; when would you like to meet?"

"I'm busy with the funeral right now, but I will get back to you when it's all settled."

After Ilsa hung up, Kat went to the window and gazed upon the rolling vine-covered hills below. She smiled. Finally, it was happening. The winery would be all theirs now. No partner.

Tuesday afternoon was a good time for Inspector Mallory and Officer Dean to visit the little town of Oliver. They knew Tuesdays were always a slow time for business, so fewer distractions as they probed. Dex was working on one side of the street, Fred the other. They could case the town faster that way.

To question people three years after a crime has been committed was a long shot, but they had tried everything else. So now they would start close to the crime scene, then work their way out in the valley.

Fred entered the Fire Hall Pub downtown and approached the bartender. "Three years ago, Sunday evening? Yeah. I probably would have been on the bar then."

"I'm looking for a tall thin guy, mustache, dark leather coat, not from around here. He drove a black Mercedes. Probably paid cash."

"That's pretty broad. No, sorry. I can't recall that."

"Okay," Fred sighed. He headed for the door when suddenly a waitress approached.

"I remember something like that."

Fred quickly came back. "Good, tell me."

"Well, there was this rude guy; he was pretty upset. That's why I remember it."

Fred took out his notebook and pen. "Go on."

"He acted creepily. He sat in the restaurant, waiting for this other guy to come and pick him up. But the guy never showed."

"Did he mention the guy's name?"

"No. He just sat here for hours and bitched. Then he had me call him a taxi. That was strange too. He wanted a ride clear back to Penticton!"

"That's great." Fred noted her name tag. "Maggie, see if you can remember the cab's name." He took out his cell. "Dex, get over to the pub. I got something."

The end of the month was nearing, the first rain had come

early, the growing season was finishing, and the last of the summer wine was in the tanks and the barrels.

Kat was now by herself in the office and tasting area. The staff was down to just the full-time workers. Uri still had much to do in the fields because there were rows of picked vines to prepare for the coming fall.

Sally was staying on full time; she was needed for the office business. That's when the call came in from Ilsa. Kat took it.

"Katerina, it's Ilsa," she began. "Can you meet me in Kelowna tomorrow? I can fly in and meet you at our bank mortgage office there. I'll send you the details."

"Of course," Kat replied. "See you there."

A short, older, modestly dressed woman met Kat and Uri in the waiting room of their mortgage office in Kelowna. The loan manager soon came out and met them.

"I'm George McDonnel," he introduced himself. They then entered his office. George quickly got down to business.

"I have prepared an intended offer of sale," he started, handing a copy to Kat and Uri. "Ilsa has proposed transferring her share of your business over to you."

Kat examined the proposal as the manager spoke.

"There is an outstanding debt against Ilsa's ownership, which she has agreed to subtract from the value of her share."

Kat and Uri read the amount of value as he spoke.

"Her share of the property has been assessed at one million seven. The amount still owing is $752,364, leaving her property assessment at just under one million."

"Furthermore," George went on, "Ilsa has agreed to price down her holdings, so the bank would accept it as a down payment for you to assume the loan." He looked up at Kat and Uri. "We consider Ilsa's offer very generous."

Ilsa spoke. "I just want to get out from under it, Kat. I've hated Honrich's irresponsible gambling. He made my life difficult, constantly hounding me to pay his debts. This sale will help me clear the board for my life and move on."

"Do you mean we can assume the additional loan with no money down?" Kat looked at George.

"Yes. But of course, your existing loan payments will increase. However, with an extended refinanced mortgage, we think that will be easily assumed."

Kat looked at Uri. He smiled. "Where do we sign?"

It was a busy day when the Vine Magazine writer and crew showed up to do a story with Gwynn. The staff was excited, especially when the photographer started wandering around, taking pictures.

Now that Kat and Uri owned the winery outright, their future was looking bright; Ann had called and informed them that sales of their wine were climbing; it had been an excellent year for Liquid Lust Winery all around.

But just as everything was rolling nicely, with a camera and staff interviews going on, an RCMP car drove up. The timing was disastrous.

Kat ushered Inspector Mallory and Officer Dean to the garden terrace. She seated the two detectives and called Uri up as they requested.

"We have some problems," Dex started sternly. "And we need straight answers from you this time."

Kat looked a bit startled. "We've cooperated with you fully Inspector."

"Have you? We believe a man named Jorge Blackmore has been up here to see you."

This was a stunning accusation, "Are you asking me?" Kat finally replied, somewhat shaken.

"Both of you. Do you know this man?"

Uri looked at Kat. "Um, no, I don't," he answered.

"Me neither," Kat also replied. "Who is he?"

"He's an associate of your deceased ex-partner. He never mentioned that name to you?"

"No," Kat answered, "He never did."

"I believe you two are not being honest with me," Dex accused them. Then the two detectives rose from the table. "We'll leave it there then, but if you two are lying to us, we'll be coming back." They turned and left.

As they drove away from the winery Fred looked over to his boss. "I think you just scared the shit out of them," he told Dex, "but it's a risky ploy. If they still don't confess to anything, we can't bring any charges."

"Yes," Dex agreed. "Hopefully, it'll rattle them enough to make some mistakes."

The rest of the morning was a time of mixed feelings for Kat. She had gone back to work, trying to keep her nerves from unraveling. The magazine photo sessions were going on. She posed with a forced smile. But when noon came, she quickly retreated to the patio, poured a glass of wine, and sat. Soon Uri was back from the fields.

"I think he knows something," Kat told him. "But if it were big, he would have pressed us more."

"He was cocksure, Kat. He will trap us, soon he'll be back."

"We buried that other body much farther away, Uri. They'll never find it."

"Kat, they found first body."

Kat pondered the situation. Why were they pressing now, all of a sudden, she wondered?

"Look, Uri," she finally answered, "there's nothing we can do. We sit tight. We may have to make plans should this escalate."

Uri went back to the fields, as Kat sat on the patio; a premonition was gripping her. She thought of the Inspector's last words. He had asked if Blackmore had been there. Uri was correct. This time they knew something.

She would wait until Uri returned, then tell him her thoughts.

It was around seven when Uri brought his tractor up. They sat at the little table by the window. It was here they had always solved their dilemmas, but this day was different. No answer was coming. She brought out the good wine, as always.

"The last of Lot-4 wine is doing well," she mentioned.

"Yes, it's good; it will bring us a nice profit soon."

"That's what I think. Let's gather the staff all together in the morning. The long weekend is coming. The staff knows the business well now."

"What are you thinking, my Kat?" Uri sensed something in her tone.

Kat reached over and poured him another glass. "Drink up Uri, I'll tell you now, and then we can discuss our future plans."

The early morning sun arose behind the eastern hills and peeked down upon the valley below. The green rows of grapevines soaked in the sun's welcoming heat, shedding the cool mist from the night's sprinkling.

Sally and the rest of the staff had arrived to take their workplaces in the winery. They had had the weekend off. They had worked hard all season, and the respite was good.

But Kat and Uri were nowhere to be seen. Sally used her keys to get into the office and found a typed note clipped to a file folder on her desk. She read the note:

Sally, please take this file, and go to the Vintner building. Once there, summon Andre and Gwynn to meet you, then take

out the notice inside and read its contents to them. Give them a
copy of the enclosed documents.
    -Signed, Kat and Uri.

Three very bewildered people had gathered in the open area of the main tank room. Sally had the folder in her hand. She opened it and took out the typed message inside, and began reading.

"As of this reading, you are all promoted to full acting managers. Andre," she looked over to him, "as well as Chief Vintner Master, you are now in charge of the fields, and all production. And Gwynn," she turned to him. "You are now the Cellar and Distributions Manager of operations."

Sally then paused to read the message addressed to herself. "Sally," she began, "I know you are reading this, so I speak to you directly. You are now in charge of all administration and the front office. I have absolute faith in you. Don't let me down."

Tears rose in Sally's eyes, as she continued reading. "Uri, and I have enclosed the notices for your salary raises and access to business transactions with our accounting firm to assist you. We are taking a leave of absence. We are still controlling owners, but we will let you share in future profits. Please keep this note and instructions confidential."

Sally looked up to the other startled employees. "Regards, Katerina and Uri Bablonski."

The three newly promoted staff sat there in shock trying to understand their sudden elevation. But they were indeed confused. Their bosses, especially Uri, were total control freaks. It was so far out of reality; it was bizarre. But they were trustworthy employees. They would honor their employer's wishes spelled out in the letter.

Chief Inspector Mallory had his own plans for the

beginning of the week. He still had a case to investigate.

"Do you have anything from that cab company, Fred?"

"No, the driver that picked Blackmore up that night retired and since then has died. Unfortunately, we have no witnesses, and the payments to him were cash. So no ID."

"We have enough to scare 'em now Fred. Let's try one more kick at the Kat."

Fred groaned at the bad pun. "It's too early; we need more time."

"No, Fred, I think we should go out again, keep the pressure on," Dex insisted. "They've had all weekend to stew. Maybe they'll crack this time."

"Alright," Fred replied, "I'll call and tell the winery we're coming." He clicked Kat's number, but Sally answered the phone.

"Hello Sally, It's Officer Dean. Would you please tell Kat that we are coming back out for another talk."

"I'm sorry, Officer Dean," Sally replied, "Kat and Uri have left on an extended vacation."

Mallory clicked off his phone, he was fuming. "They've run on us," he ranted. "Damn it, Freddy, you check with the airlines. I'll call the border. We should have pulled their passports."

Fred brought up the airlines on his computer. He knew Uri and Katerina were Chechen citizens. He scanned the scheduled flights for the Chechen Republic.

"Okay, I got it!" He yelled. Dex came quickly over. "There was a KLM flight that left Vancouver Saturday for Amsterdam. Then it connected to Grozny, in the Chechen Republic. I'll call the airline and ask if they were on it."

Fred reached the KLM desk, gave them the names, and waited, nodded his head then hung up. He looked up to Dex.

"Sorry boss, they're probably walking the streets of Grozny right now."

102

"Dammit! Alright then," Dex groaned, "we'll get more info. We'll expedite their asses for unlawful flight."

"Sorry, Dex," Fred replied, shaking his head. "Canada has no extradition treaty with the Chechen Republic."

Vine Magazine was out now, and the Liquid Lust Winery was the hot topic in the valleys wine chatter. Sally was extra busy. She had used her new authority to hire further help for the tasting patio.

Over at police HQ in Penticton, Fred Dean stared at the pile of case studies he had on the Honrich murder case. They had found the Mercedes, its stripped, ravaged hulk discovered in a pile of other heaps, at a dump site. But they had found no additional evidence.

Mary Defoe had advised they keep the case open, but they still didn't have an actual charge. As to the winery, without a case, they couldn't impound it. And the ownership had been transferred over to the employees anyway. The winery continued to flourish.

Andre LeShan's favorite time of day was late afternoon after work. He loved to sit and read the wine news of famous vineyards from around the world. It had been three years now since Uri and Kat had left, and he always hoped he might discover some news on their new life in their far-off world.

One day he was looking to see who had claimed the World Wine Enthusiast award for that year.

And there it was.

The first place prize had gone to a new winery from the Chechen Republic. The owners, Uri and Katerina Bablonski, had fought a tough battle for their share of the market against the local Oligarch. But, they were finally successful in bottling their new Chardonnay. As of this writing, their rival subsequently left and hasn't been located.

He read on, the article's writer likened the winner to a prized bottle he had found in Canada, labeled Uri's Full-Bodied-Special Reserve.

He described the winning wine as a bold, meaty taste.

THE LAST REQUIEM

When the Maestro appeared, the packed theater burst into applause. He strode across the stage and took his position at center. The clapping grew louder; cheering soon followed. The Music Director came to the podium, and the audience quieted.

"Ladies and gentlemen," he began. "Maestro Langdon Wallinski will now play Concerto Number One from his renowned music score for the soundtrack, Requiem for a Fantasy."

Total silence.

The Maestro raised his bow and nodded to the piano accompanist to his side. The pianist began slowly, repeatedly striking a single note, softly introducing the coming theme's melody. Now came the flowing, sweet song of the violin.

The sound grew stronger, rising in intensity until the piano, following the violin, filled the theater. The music winged upward, a soaring majestic bird. With each pull of the string, the instrument held the Maestro completely under its spell, his face twisting and agonizing under its commanding grip. On and on, the powerful sound continued. There seemed no end; and no beginning; rising, ebbing, issuing a story that begged to be known. At last, the piece began its final descent, falling once again onto a single fading note. Then total silence.

The entire theater burst into a rousing ovation. The

violinist brought down his bow and held the instrument in both arms, clutching it tightly to his chest in a lover's embrace. It was a powerful, moving gesture.

The Maestro then abruptly left the stage; enormous cheering and applause followed him off.

After several minutes, the audience quieted down to a low chatter. Anticipation built for the violinist's return for the next part of the Requiem. Minutes passed, but still, the Maestro had not appeared.

Then, a loud gunshot!

The sound resounded from somewhere behind the stage, shocking the house into silence. The music director immediately jumped up and ran back towards the dressing rooms. Nervous chatter filled the auditorium. The startled gathering waited for the drama of the shot to unfold. The theater's manager soon came to the stage and asked for quiet.

"Ladies and gentlemen," he told them, "We are so sorry to inform you that there has been an incident backstage. The rest of the concert is now canceled. We will return your tickets as soon as possible. Thank you." He turned and left.

Cindy William's cell phone always had urgent calls. But this one had a New York City prefix and the name Wallinski. That certainly got her attention. It was a name familiar to anyone who followed the music scene. She instantly called back.

"This is Ann," an older woman's voice answered.

"Hello, Ann, this is Cindy Williams. You had left a message on my cell."

"Yes, thank you for calling back, Cindy. I'm Ann Wallinski, Landon Wallinski's sister."

"Oh, dear! I heard about the tragic incident at the concert. So sorry to learn about your brother's death."

"It's actually not so surprising, Cindy. Langdon has had

many emotional problems over the years."

"What can I do for you, Ann?"

"I would like your professional help. I hear you are well known for your work in suicide cases in the Dallas area."

"Ann, I must tell you I'm only a counselor; I have no medical degree. I may not be the person you want."

"You are the only one left, Cindy. I've tried many experts, but no one can help me. It's been a week now since Langdon's death, and I've gotten nowhere. But I've read so much about you and your success in suicide cases."

"Ok, but tell me, what is it you expect from me? I'm just a social worker in mental health."

"Oh, it's not for me, Cindy. It's for my other brother, Quentin."

"Quentin Wallinski? I've never heard that name. How is he involved?"

"He was mixed up in a scandal over six years ago and then he disappeared. The last I heard, he was in the Dallas area. But he can't be found. I don't even know if he's still alive."

"What can you tell me about that incident?"

"There was a death in the family—Langdon's wife, Alexia. There were rumors she had an affair with Quentin. Then, several months after the alleged incident, she took her own life."

"How did that accusation affect the two brothers?"

"We have no proof, and they both denied that anything ever happened. But Alexia was a stunning beauty with a somewhat wild reputation. And Quentin was always around, so it's not too hard to believe."

"But if they both denied this, why did the two men drift then apart?"

"It mainly was Quentin. They were both struggling musicians living in Greenwich Village. But when Langdon introduced his composition, it took off. Then Hollywood used the piece for a hit movie, and he became instantly famous. Quentin, however, struggled with his work and became depressed. His career faded, and he soon disappeared. We never saw him again. As for Langdon, he never got over Alexia's death. That's probably why he finally took his life."

"But, Ann, Langdon's been playing the piece for over six years. Why now?"

"Actually, Cindy, he had to go under psychiatric counsel before every concert. Playing that score took him to the edge. It made him famous, but it finally destroyed him."

"Ann, I must tell you. I can't promise anything. I work with Texas mental health services and their resources are limited."

"Please, Cindy." Ann's voice began breaking up. "Quentin is all that remains of my family. You're my last hope."

Cindy was very familiar with the Dallas holding facilities for street people. She had worked with many suicide cases from the area. But in this case the officer in charge was of little help.

"Quentin Wallinski? Yeah, a guy named Quentin has been in and out of here a lot, but we've released him."

This was no surprise to Cindy. Derelicts, druggies, and mental cases were a real problem for jail holding areas. They would disturb regular prisoners, and the staff hated cleaning up after them. They were put back on the street as soon as possible.

"Do you have an address?"

"No, he's a street bum. You'll probably find him living near downtown around Greenville Ave. That's where a lot of the low life hang out."

"Can you provide a description? Any pics?"

"Yes, here's his rap sheet with habits, and a recent photo."

If city streets are arteries, then Greenville Avenue would

be Dallas's lower colon. But it's an intestine of trouble, starting from midtown and running east out to the fringe—a stretch of rundown lower-income apartment buildings and bars with a history of crime and drug addiction.

But Greenville is also a colorful part of Dallas's past. It once was the fashionable nightclub district of the city. It is here, at Greenville and Park Lane, where a famous old filling station still sits from the thirties. The same station Bonnie and Clyde used to fill their soon-to-be-shot-up Ford just before sheriff deputies famously ambushed them. Not far down the street, Jack Ruby, the assassin of Lee Harvey Oswald, once owned a small bar and club.

Cindy parked her car near downtown and began walking east past Greenville's now dilapidated, old buildings. Her slim, attractive frame was now draped in coarse, billowy-fitting clothes. She wore no make-up and her hair was tied back. It was a trick she had learned the hard way when tracking street people in dangerous areas.

There were many little food shops gracing the street. These were the usual areas where derelicts begged for change. Cindy went from place one place to the next, asking around with little luck until she came to a tiny fruit kiosk on the corner, owned by an elderly Vietnamese man.

"Ah, sure, I know him. He comes here sometimes. He's a good guy, but still trouble. He steals; I give him apples, so he does not steal from me."

"Where does he usually stay?"

"You try down under the freeway overpass. Street people go there all the time."

Cindy knew that area. It was the absolute bottom for the most desperate lost souls, both the innocent and the evil. She knew she would be ok in the daylight, but would never go there alone at night.

She made her way down a steep embankment and began walking along the large foul-smelling drainage ditch, carefully avoiding discarded refuse and squalor. It wasn't long before she spotted a man fitting Quentin's description. He was sitting next to one of the tall concrete pillars that held up the noisy freeway above. She moved closer and closer, until she was sure it was him.

"Hello, Quentin." She said. "My name is Cindy."

He was sickly and frail, with a myriad of bruises and cuts over his arms. From the look of the rips and tears in his filthy pants, his legs were probably in the same shape. Cindy could tell immediately that he wasn't a druggie—no needle marks. It looked like he was going to get up and walk away. Cindy backed off a bit. "Hey, no need to leave; I'm a friend."

He stared up, his sunburnt face half-covered by a knotted, dirty beard. "I don't need any friends."

"You must have some out here."

"What the hell is good about friends? They are useless; they just want something from you."

"Your sister wants you."

Quentin's eyes narrowed. "My sister? How do you know her? I'm an outcast, a scourge on the family."

"She called me. I work with welfare services."

"Why me?"

"It's what your sister wants. I don't know you. It's her I'm trying to help. You can lie out here and rot like a dead pigeon for all I care."

The statement seemed to stun Quentin; he looked surprised. "Well, how about that? The first God damn honest person I've met."

"Why don't you take my cell and talk to her? What have you got to lose?"

"I'm a disappointment to her. Why should she care?"

Cindy knelt on the concrete and faced the man. "Well, I talked to her, and I didn't hear that. Tell me why I'm wrong?"

"I'm a disaster. How could she like me? Look at me, look at where I am? I belong here."

"They tell me you have a talent in music like your brother. Is that true?"

"Musical talent? My brother tell you that?"

This was a shocker; he didn't know his brother was dead! Cindy had to stop and carefully weigh her next questions.

"Did Langdon really tell you all those things?"

"He didn't have to say it. I knew what I had become. I knew I couldn't measure up to him. He was the success, and I was the outcast brother."

"Is that why you stopped playing, quit your violin?"

"No, the violin quit me. I could not play it anymore."

"Tell me, Quentin. I have on record that you tried to take your life many times. Tell me now. Why?"

Anger suddenly welled up in the man. He stood up, frightening Cindy, and smashed his fist hard into the concrete pillar.

"SEE these HANDs!" he yelled, holding them up to her. "They have no talent. I possess no skill. I'll never be like him. Never! I am not worthy of the man." His right hand was bleeding, damaged from the blow. Cindy tried not to show shock. She carefully stood up and asked to look at his wound.

Quentin pulled it back. "It's just a hand; it has no special meaning."

It was clear there was a different problem here. "Ok, please talk with me. You hate yourself. Why?"

"I need to die. What is the purpose for me to be here? I've nothing to offer but disgust. And it's ripping me apart inside."

"I'll not ask you for hate's reason. I'll ask you for the way for you to get by it."

"As long as my brother is alive I must bear it. That's my

111

reason. Now you leave me alone. GO! Get away from me!"

It was time now to tell Quentin his brother was gone, but how would he react?

"Quentin, listen to me carefully now. I have something to tell you. Will you promise me you won't do anything rash?"

"There is nothing that could make me promise that."

"Your brother is dead. He took his life a week ago after playing the opening piece from the Requiem."

Quentin's face turned ghastly white. He stood, saying nothing, his mouth agape. Then he leaned back against the pillar and slowly sank to the concrete. He put his head in his hands and cried. Cindy sat down on the concrete beside him.

"Why? Why him first?" He blurted out. "It should have been me."

The two sat in the squalid ditch for a time, saying nothing to each other. Cindy felt it would be best if she remained silent.

Quentin finally spoke. "I didn't mean to kill her."

"Who?"

"Alexia. It was all my doing."

"What happened?"

"I was with Alexia in their apartment when Langdon caught us. I tried to reason with him, convince him this was only an affair—I'd leave New York and never come back. But then Alexia screamed at me—you liar! We both planned to leave Langdon. Tell him that!" She ran wailing into the bedroom and slammed the door."

"What did your brother do?"

"Langdon went into a blinding rage. I tried to convince him that I had started the affair, which I hadn't, but I thought I could save his marriage. I told him that I would leave, go away, and never see Alexia again."

"Did he believe you?"

"He called me every name in the gutter, told me I was a

Judas. That I had no conscience, that I was a thief. I agreed with him; I was the worst traitor on the earth for what I had done. Then I did the unthinkable. I told Langdon I would give him my new concerto, which I had just written. I took the music score from my briefcase and put it on the coffee table. This is my gift to you, I told him. Then I left. I never saw him or Alexia again."

Now Cindy had heard it all. But she needed to address this killing of Alexia. "Why blame yourself for her suicide, Quentin? You weren't even there."

"Oh, but I was, Cindy. She called me many times after I left, asking me if we could make it work, tell me that she didn't love Langdon. But I could not tell her how much I loved her. Instead, I lied, tried to convince her to stay with Langdon, that I would not ruin my brother's marriage."

"Then did she stop?"

Quentin fought to control his voice. "She tried to call me again over the following months, but I didn't answer. Then, she left me a final heartbreaking message. She was distraught, could not go on with Langdon. The next day, I received the terrible news. Alexia had leaped from the twenty-first floor of their downtown apartment. That's when I left New York for good."

Now it was all out. This man had carried his love and his guilt for this woman's death all these years. "The Requiem," Cindy asked. "Was that the score you gave Langdon? You wrote it for Alexia, didn't you?"

"Yes, but only I, and now you, must ever know that."

"You wrote it with such power. How is it a love song?"

"It's the deep sorrow of an empty heart, pounding out its aching pain, longing for something it can never have."

"Listen to me, Quentin, this is a tragic story, but it's not just about you. Langdon didn't have to take that music score.

He didn't have to say it was his. He lied! His sin was as great as yours. And Alexia, she enticed you into that affair, and she is equally guilty. Don't you see Quentin? There are no villains here, only victims!"

"No. I live on, and they are both dead. It's my fault. All mine! I gave him the Requiem as a gift to absolve myself for my sin, but the piece became a curse instead. It became a millstone around his neck that he carried always, reminding him of Alexia's crushed body lying in the street. I put that curse upon him."

Cindy reached her arms forward and grabbed the man's shoulders, and shook him. "NO, YOU DIDN'T! There is no curse, only guilt. He put that guilt upon himself by taking it. It's all divided equally among you. Death has taken two of you. Now it's just you and your sister. Do not pull her down too. Be there for her and save the fourth person in this story."

"I, I couldn't bear her death too."

"Come with me now, Quentin. Ann loves you. You're all she has left. She has grieved for you all these years. You can make everything right through her."

"I cannot." He shook his head. "I will deny every word I've told you here today."

"The Requiem is safe in the hands of your brother's legacy. I truly believe he loved you for that. We can leave it there for him."

"But I can't go back. I belong here; it's become my place in life."

"NO! It isn't your place! It's an excuse for running away. Don't you see Quentin? You can't hide from your guilt, but you can deal with it in time. I can get you a room in health services." Cindy looked at his swollen, bleeding hand. "You need a doctor; your hand's broken. Will you at least do that? Please!"

Quentin looked away from Cindy; she could see he was

fighting the request. Finally, he nodded. "Yes, I will go."

So the two people in the ditch under the freeway began walking up the dirty causeway, back towards the city.

With Cindy's constant visiting and encouragement, Quentin was finally certified fit to leave the care facility. She then found him a room in a hostel with money Ann had sent for him. Several more months of counseling followed. Over time he recovered enough to return to his sister. That was a banner day. That was the day Cindy put him on Amtrak to New York City. He now appeared ready to face his past world, with his sister's help and further care.

Cindy would receive encouraging texts from him from time to time; then a year later, a phone call. She knew this was important. She quickly answered.

"Hi, Cindy," Quentin's voice sounded much more robust and positive than the sickly man she had placed on the train. "Guess what? I'm playing again, and I think I may even have some work."

"That's fantastic, Quentin. I knew you would."

"Yeah, but I put it down to my last name. That's what opened the door."

"Well, listen, the door opened, but with your talent, you will keep it open."

"I've got a problem, though, Cindy. They want me to play The Requiem. I, I don't think I can do it."

"You can, Quentin. Get it past you. It's best if you faced your demons. Remember, the music still has its beauty, and everyone who hears it will place their own personal experiences within it. Channel yours to the good things that can happen now."

"Ok, I'll think about it. I certainly can use the gig."

"Do it, Quentin. In fact, you have to. It will never go away until you face it."

Three weeks later, Cindy got a text from Quentin: Good news, I'm playing my first recital of the Requiem on June 1, at 8: pm on PBS. It will help me if I know you're watching.

She texted back: Of course! I will be honored. Cindy.

The excitement of the audience was noticeable as Quentin appeared. He was walking straight and tall as he crossed the stage and took his place at the center. After the applause quieted down, Quentin took the mike and spoke.

"Everyone," he began, "Thank you for coming and putting your faith in my attempt at my brother's masterpiece. Playing this piece had become difficult for Langdon for personal reasons. But now it's my turn to play it. As you may have heard, I've had a hard road to arrive here myself, but I could not have survived that journey without a special person who saved me. This piece was originally written for someone else, but I want to dedicate it to another. This person is listening now, and I want her to know every note of this composition is just for her."

When the concert was over, Cindy clicked off the TV and sat in silence.

Cindy Williams, it is said, was the toughest worker in suicide watch. She had seen horror and death most of her adult life, working with victims in the most tragic cases. But today she watched a ten-minute music composition on PBS, and when it was over, for the first time in her career, she broke down and cried.

FLIGHT TO FAIRBANKS

Will brought the aircraft's nose up to face the horizon of the western mountains. The air was clear, the visibility not bad for a night flight. He set the altimeter for eight thousand feet and settled back in his seat.

"What time do you see us getting in?" Jean asked.

"We should make it in around ten."

"Good," she replied. "When we're close, I'll text Mom and dad, tell them we're back."

Will and Jean McLain were returning from a visit to his father's cabin up in the high country. Will was a ferry pilot for a local mining company and they had granted him the use of their aircraft for this brief vacation. The time away had been enjoyable, but now they needed to get back to their jobs in Fairbanks, where their small child, Darlene, was staying with Jean's parents.

The late evening mountain air began rising now, making the flight's ascent a bit choppy. That's good, Will thought, hardly a cloud in sight. It would be smooth sailing back to Fairbanks.

All of a sudden, THUD! THUD! The plane lurched violently as objects out of nowhere slammed into the windshield.

"Oh, my God!" Jean screamed.

Will grabbed the yoke with both hands and fought to steady the lurching aircraft. Blood and parts of birds splattered on the glass, the engine sputtered, the airplane pitched sideways. Will fought for control as the horizon disappeared from view. He struggled to bring the nose back to level flight.

"Will, I'm hurt!" Jean blurted out. Will looked over and noticed blood running from her nose; she had hit her head against the front panel.

"OH NO! Are you all right?" Will reached across and touched her shoulder.

"I'll be okay; don't worry about me. What happened?"

"We hit a flock of geese on our climb."

Now the engine began vibrating violently, "Dammit," Will cursed. "The prop's damaged!" He reached forward and hit the kill switch.

Silence.

No sound now except for the whistling air over the wings.

Will could see Jean was gasping for air, trying to breathe; she was in obvious pain. "Jean, are you sure you're alright?"

"Yes, yes. I'll get the emergency kit and pack my nose. You just fly."

Will organized his thoughts. They were in extreme danger—a glider now, with no power, and at night over the rough Alaskan terrain. 'Don't panic,' he told himself, Find a landing spot.

He scanned the ground for an emergency landing, but it was too dark and rocky. Now he realized they were in serious trouble. There was no safe place anywhere to land. He grabbed up the radio mike and clicked the switch.

"MAYDAY! MAYDAY! Cessna 172, flight N209, loss of power, emergency landing!"

There was no answer! He clicked again. "I repeat, MAY…"

"Flight 209. State your position," came a calm male voice.

"We are forty-five miles south of Channing Lake, gliding at 5500 feet, two people on board."

"Do you have any visual at all?"

"Very little, too dark. We need the nearest airport immediately."

"Okay, Flight 209, now listen. I'm at Langdon Field, approximately fifteen miles from your position. Do you have any instrument landing systems?"

"No, we are strictly visual reference, standard instruments. I will need flight guidance."

"Alright, 209. We'll work on that. You must conserve your descent."

"Roger that Langdon Field. Can you give me a heading?"

The radio was silent for a moment, then the voice returned, "Flight 209, turn left to 195 degrees, maintain decent at level glide."

"Langdon, that's a long glide. Are you sure we can make that?"

The male voice was calm but concerned, "Flight 209, who am I talking to?"

"I'm Will; my wife Jean is with me."

"Will, this is Joe Danforth. I'm going to get you down. You stay calm. We're going to do this together."

The sudden change in conversation was disconcerting. It appeared Joe was not sure they could make it.

"What's he saying?" Jean interrupted, her voice frightened. "Will, are we going to crash land?"

"Look, Honey, we're okay; this guy sounds like he's a pro. We'll make it."

But Will knew it was almost impossible. At their lower altitude, they would be miles short. Will steadied his nerves; he put the thought away and focused on the glide.

Joe came back on the line, "Will, look below and to your right. Do you see a small lake?"

"Yes, Joe, due north."

"That's a good sign. Listen, there's a small mountain range to your right, glide sixty degrees right, then turn back to your heading."

"What's he doing, Will?" Jean blurted out. "Shouldn't we stay straight?"

"He's taking us over an updraft, honey; it will give us more altitude. This guy knows these mountains."

Joe came back again as if he had overheard their conversation, "Jean," he said, his voice reassuring, "I will get you in. Do you have any children?"

The face of Jean's young daughter flashed into her mind. "Oh, yes, Darlene. She's five. She starts school soon."

"Jean, I have a daughter too, her name's Kate. She lives not far from here. But don't worry, you will see Darlene again. I promise you."

Somehow, Jean's panic subsided. She felt better, almost as if they were already on the ground, safely down, even though the air rushing past the silent aircraft said differently.

Will studied the approaching terrain, but now it was so dark that all he could see was the profile of the horizon. Fear rose in his gut; they were committed now. If his glide was too high or too low—he shook the terrible thought from his mind.

Now the dark outline of distant mountains grew closer. Will could make out the lights of structures passing under the descending aircraft; he clicked on the mike. "Joe, I think we're over some small buildings."

"Great. You're on the outer perimeter. What's your altitude?"

"320 feet."

"Okay. A road will come up soon: it has streetlights. Maintain glide."

Will could see the lights coming up fast. Then, to his horror, he could make out electrical wires between the poles. He was heading straight at them.

"Joe!" Will yelled in the mike, "Wires! Wires!"

"Maintain glide. Do not change course!" Joe yelled back.

Will's hands froze on the yoke as the wires loomed up dangerously close and then passed just below the wheels. Up ahead, the scarcely discernible runway.

"Joe, I can't make out the strip."

"You're over it now. FULL FLAPS!"

Will reached between the seats and yanked the flap lever back. The aircraft flared out; the back wheels banged onto the ground. He pushed down hard on the foot pedals, and the plane slid down the dark runway. Then, at last, it came to a stop.

They were down.

Will snapped opened his door and ran around to the other side, helping his shaken wife from her seat. "I'm okay," she told him. "Just let me rest; I think I may have a broken nose."

A police car's red light flashed, the headlights of the car lighting up the scene as it drew nearer.

"Are you alright?" An Office enquired as he rushed over.

"We're fine, Officer," Will replied, "but my wife will need some medical attention."

"No problem, I'll drive you to our local medic."

Jean was being attended to for her injury at the small clinic; Will sat nearby. The police officer came and sat beside him.

"Wow," the man told him. "It was pitch black out there. When I spotted you gliding in with no power, I thought you were a goner for sure, how'd' you find that unlit runway?"

"We were lucky alright. But it was the guy in the tower that got us down."

"Tower?" The police officer replied. "What tower?"

"The guy in the airport tower," Will replied. "He talked us all the way in."

The officer put his hand on Will's shoulder. "Sir, that

airport has been closed for years; there's no one in that tower. It's abandoned."

"But that's impossible," Will said in disbelief. "He talked me in all the way. He saved our lives."

"Who talked you in, sir? What was this guy's name?"

"He said his name was Joe, Joe Danforth."

"Oh, my God! Sir, listen to me. Joe Danforth died over 20 years ago."

"No," Will cried. "He is alive. Jean and I both talked to him."

"Mr. McLain, that can't be. Joe Danforth and his wife were both killed after their aircraft's engine lost oil pressure. He was trying to make it back to this very airport when he crashed into the side of a mountain up near the lake. Sir, I know this for a fact; I was in the crew that brought their bodies in."

"Officer!" came Jean's voice from the other room, "Joe had a young daughter named Kate, didn't he?"

"Why yes, ma'am, he did. How did you know that?"

"Joe told me so himself, Officer, just before we landed."

A KILLING ON THE 16th TEE

Ron and Kevin eyed the large man in the blue flowery shirt descending the hill.

"Expensive clubs," Ron observed.

"Yeah," Kevin replied, taking a practice swing, his club nipping the top of the grass. "Probably custom-made."

Ron shielded his eyes from the bright mid-morning sun. As the man drew closer, he could hear his footsteps crunching in the loose gravel of the pathway.

"He doesn't look familiar," Ron noted, his voice a little lower. "What's he shooting?"

"His caddy says he shot 86," Kevin answered, moving a little closer to Ron, "and he cheated to get that." Kevin took another swing. "Rich, too," he added. "The word around is he's got cash up his ass."

The man was almost upon them now, his big cart banging along behind him. Ron eyed the man's huge golf bag. It was crammed with every gee-gaw a neophyte golfer would buy. "This is gonna be a turkey shoot," Ron quietly snickered.

"Excellent day for a round, eh?" the man announced as he approached, sticking out his hand. "I'm George Norman."

Ron smiled and took his hand. "No relation to Greg, I hope?"

George laughed, revealing perfect white teeth against his

tanned face. "Only in my dreams," he replied. "And you are?"

"Ron Jakes, and this is Kevin Brown."

Kevin reached over to shake George's hand, noticing the big gold Rolex on his wrist. "I haven't seen you around the club before, George. Did you just join?"

"Well, actually, I'm only in town for a while," George allowed. "A friend of mine on the committee loaned me his card to get in a few rounds."

Ron shouldered his bag as they began walking. "I hope you don't mind if we don't use caddies, George," Ron mentioned. "The club, um, frowns on the sporting game here, if you know what I mean."

"Not at all, gentlemen," George replied with a big grin. "I also like playing on a professional course without carts—it's more like the big boys game."

George set his overloaded golf bag on the first tee. He pulled out a driver. "Well, gentlemen, what's the going rate for sportsmen here, anyway?"

Ron gave Kevin a sly glance; they'd already decided to give George double the standard bet.

"How about three hundred a hole?"

George grinned. "That'll do for a start." He made a sweeping gesture to the fairway. "You first."

Ron took his stance firmly at the tee, fixed his eyes down the course, brought his club back, and unleashed his swing. His driver came down smooth, striking the ball with a loud crack and sending it straight down the fairway.

"Very good!" George exclaimed. "They told me to watch out for you."

Ron smiled to himself. Actually, it was one of the poorer drives he'd made on this hole.

The threesome played on, and the scores were close. But by the time they reached the seventh tee, George had yet to win a hole. He took out a handkerchief, wiped his brow, and turned to the other two golfers.

"Let's up the bet."

Ron grinned at Kevin; they had been waiting for this. "What have you got in mind, George?"

"How about a thousand a hole?" George replied without batting an eye.

Ron almost gasped. Nobody played for that kind of money. He glanced over at Kevin, who had turned white as a ghost. "Did you say a thousand dollars?"

"That's what I said. You guys can cover that, can't you?"

Ron had to ponder this for a moment. Was George trying to hustle them? If they lost, they'd be wiped out. But what if George was used to waging this kind of money? Maybe it was peanuts to him. They could make a killing. Ron glanced over at Kevin for a sign. Kevin looked nervous as hell. But after some thought, he gave Ron the nod.

"All right, George," Ron replied. "You're on!"

The morning sun rose higher, shrinking the shadows beneath the tall sycamores that flanked the fairways. But the added heat did nothing for George's game. Ron and Kevin, however, had improved noticeably. Now they were hitting the ball deep in the fairway and chipping to the fat of the greens. By the time they reached the fifteenth tee, George was down for over ten thousand dollars.

Next to the tee area was an inviting fountain. George found a shaded bench nearby and slumped down on it to rest and sip from the cool water. His face was now bright red from the midday sun. He had chucked all the excess golf paraphernalia from his cart three holes back. He took out a handkerchief and wiped his brow again.

"Okay, gentlemen," George announced, "why don't we

make this game much more interesting?"

"You want to play for more?" Kevin blurted out, trying to conceal his excitement.

"I've got something else in mind," George replied. "I'm proposing a whole new game."

Above the course at the clubhouse parking lot sat a huge silver Bentley. The car loomed like a fat moored yacht among the lesser vehicles. As the three men approached the car, one of them fished in his pocket for his keys.

"Ah, yes, here it is," George announced, opening the car's trunk. Ron and Kevin peered over his shoulder as he took out an expensive leather briefcase and snapped it open. George removed an envelope from the case and held it up for the two men.

"I have here a cashier's check," he announced. "It's made out for the sum of Two Million Dollars at a local bank. All I have to do is write your name on it, and it's yours."

The two men's eyes grew wide as pancakes as George handed them the envelope.

"Let's waive the paltry ten thousand I owe you," George went on. "Let's play a golf game for real money." Ron removed the check and the two men studied it carefully. It seemed genuine enough.

"Good God, man!" Ron sputtered as he handed it back to George. "Are you freaking wacko? I don't know what anybody's told you, George, but we can't raise that kind of money."

"Oh, you don't have to put up a dime," George came back. "I'll do all the paying, but I'll just be a spectator. You'll be playing each other."

Near the sixteenth tee is a thick copse of woods that offers complete privacy to all but the most errant of golfers. Down through a wooded little trail came George, leading the two men. Soon he turned off the path, and they entered through the leafy branches until they came upon a bit of a clearing.

"Right here, gentlemen," George announced, motioning to the open space, "is where I propose we play out our golf drama. Here it will begin, and here it will end."

"END?" Kevin blurted out.

"Oh, yes." George's voice now became grave. "I propose you two play the sixteenth hole, and only the sixteenth hole, for two million dollars. When it's over, we will return here to this clearing where the winner will receive the check, and the loser will pay the penalty."

Kevin didn't like the sound of that, but before he could speak, Ron was all over George.

"What are you, some kind of creeping pervert?" Ron yelled in George's face.

"Gentlemen, I assure you," George replied, "this game is way beyond some simple sadistic contest. What I'm talking about is on a much higher level than that. I'm suggesting a decisive competition of the highest challenge. The ultimate sport."

Ron was appalled. "I don't want any part of this," he snapped. "I don't know what the hell you're getting to, George, but you can pay up what you owe me NOW!"

Kevin grabbed Ron's arm. "Wait, let's at least hear him out. He's talking two million dollars."

Ron stared at George menacingly. "Okay, make it quick, then I'm out of here."

George began walking around the clearing, waving his arms like a salesperson at a seminar.

"Think of it, gentlemen," he suggested, "both of you today will have a fifty-fifty chance of walking off this course a multi-millionaire. Haven't you always dreamed of having that kind of money?" He paused for effect. "Well, it can be yours.

No more hustling for scraps to play golf. No more wondering if you will ever be anything other than penny-anti golf bums. You will travel the world, see it all. Play the best courses in every country." He held the tantalizing check in front of the two men's faces. "Whose name shall I sign on it?"

Kevin looked at the check; he shook his head as if to make it disappear. "You said the loser would pay a penalty. I think you better explain that."

George reached into his jacket pocket and pulled out a bundle of purple velvet. He unwrapped the folds to reveal a small silver-plated Derringer. He opened the breach and inserted a stubby bullet, and snapped it shut.

"This, gentlemen," he soberly announced as he held the gun for them to see, "will be the loser's fate!"

Ron and Kevin stared at the Derringer in stunned silence. Now it was clear. George was implying cold-blooded murder!

"You're willing to pay two million dollars to shoot the loser of a golf game?" Ron stammered.

"Oh, no, not me," George answered. "The winner would do that."

Ron looked at George in disbelief. "You're insane!"

"Insanity is relative," George replied. "How many people go to auto races hoping to see the drivers splatter their guts all over the track? Are they insane? No. They go for the thrill of the danger. It's the element of death, Mr. Jakes—that's what makes a contest exciting. It's as old as the Coliseum in ancient Rome."

"Yes, the racetracks are dangerous," Ron came back, "but the drivers don't agree beforehand to kill each other. If it happens, it's accidental. It's not a God damn, deliberate killing."

"But it's still there, Mr. Jakes, that possibility of death. The competitors will do anything to win, and the spectators know it. That's what I am—a paying spectator."

"Wait a minute," Kevin interrupted. "This is ridiculous. Someone will hear the shot. We'd be charged with murder."

George held up the weapon again. "It's a small caliber, no one will hear it, and as for the body," he smiled, "they'll find the gun in the victim's hand—an apparent suicide."

"This is crazy!" Kevin blurted out, turning away. "I want no part of this."

"Really? Two million dollars is a significant amount of money. Are you crazy enough to turn it down? One of you will be set for life." George waited for a reaction.

"That's why you're doing this?" Ron said. "For the excitement?"

"Yes, of course," George answered, as if the question was obvious. "I've traveled the world looking for the ultimate sport. The money's nothing to me; I'm a wealthy man. I'll pay anything for that one blood-rushing moment of life or death in the arena."

George sensed they were listening. "The challenge, gentlemen, think of it. You're sportsmen, will you enter that arena? Do you have what it takes to play in the ultimate game?"

Kevin turned to face George, his voice now becoming lower and colder. "The winner gets the money today?"

"I'll drive him to the bank myself," George answered.

"Wait one god-damn minute here," Ron barged in. "How do we know you won't fudge the deal? You can renege at any time. It's the winner's word against yours. Who in the hell would believe this story?"

"AHA!" George shot back. "You've touched on the nub of this affair—the turning point, if you will." He pulled a miniature recorder out of his shirt pocket. "I've recorded everything we've said in this meeting. All the damning evidence is here in our voices. Once the end game is completed, the winner gets the recording as the deal sealer. We both would have much to lose should this agreement ever become known."

George now emphasized his next words carefully. "This then is the juncture. We must now make a critical decision. Do I erase this device, and we walk out of here, or do we play?"

Ron looked over at Kevin, but Kevin said nothing—he turned back to George. "Answer me now, damn you, are you this committed? Are you this serious?"

George held the check up one more time. "I can tell you now that I'm all in, Mr. Jakes. For you, it's all about the money, but it's the end game for me. That's what I'm paying for, and I wouldn't miss it for anything."

George then went and sat upon an up-rooted stump and waited for the men's decision.

The two men began arguing. Soon it became clear they were talking themselves into the bargain more than they were talking themselves out of it. Finally, after much discussion, they broke off and stood apart. Now George knew he had them. With the decision near, the two men both realized they were now mortal enemies—obstacles in each other's path to the coveted check. Losing was unthinkable. Survival was all that mattered to each man now.

It was Kevin who agreed first. The money George was proposing was his lifetime dream, but Ron still resisted. The thought of killing a man was too extreme. He couldn't imagine doing it. But God, he wanted that money, and the odds were good. He was the better player of the two men. At one time, Ron had almost earned his pro card. But then again, Kevin was no slouch, and anything might happen on only one hole.

Finally, after a gut-wrenching ten minutes, Ron raised his eyes to meet George's. "All right, you sick bastard," he said. "Let's play!"

The par four sixteenth was the most challenging hole on the course. Most players needed five shots, or more, to complete it. The fairway ran two hundred and thirty yards out, and then doglegged sharply right for two hundred yards to the green. A long drive would overshoot the dogleg and find the trees. A short drive would leave the golfer in front of another stand of woods with no chance to the hole.

Ron won the coin toss and elected to drive first. He placed his tee and took his stance. He felt his nerves creeping in. He had won many a dollar at this hole, but now he stared down its menacing fairway in fear. This time the stakes would be much higher, the penalty much more severe.

"Focus, damn you!" Ron whispered to himself as he stood frozen over the ball. Then he unleashed his swing. The ball ripped high off the tee and soared past the first group of trees. It carried straight, and dropped dead center into the mouth of the dogleg and rolled to a perfect lie.

"Bravo!" George shouted. "Bravo!"

Now it was Kevin's turn at the tee. He was shaking noticeably. He was the underdog, and he knew it. A bad swing here, and it was over. He gripped the club tightly and gathered all his strength for the drive of his life. He stood frozen over the ball for what seemed an eternity, then he brought down his driver, and the ball streaked away.

Kevin realized it was a slice as soon as he hit it. The ball climbed high towards the dogleg, but then began turning towards the trees.

"Come on! Come on!" Kevin screamed as the ball sailed towards disaster. It dropped dangerously close to the front of the woods, bounced back to the fairway, and barely dribbled into the dogleg opening.

"By God, I think you made it," George shouted with excitement.

"You're enjoying this, aren't you, you freaking bastard!" Kevin snapped at George, slamming his club back into his bag.

As Kevin approached his ball, he saw he had a clear shot at the flag, but a treacherous trap lay between his ball and the green. However, Ron's lie was farther past the opening, and although further from the hole, it offered him a much better angle to the tee, with no trap to clear. Ron was away.

Ron was confident now as he stood over his ball. He would disconnect his mind from his body and let his natural swing take over. Ron stood over the ball, brought his iron down smoothly, picked the ball from the turf, and sent it flying down the second dogleg. It carried high to the flag, plopped down in the center of the green, and rolled to less than five feet from the pin. He could be down in a sure birdie three!

Kevin had to stand in shock as George whooped and hollered in a loud outburst of jubilation. Now, he must ignore Ron's perfect shot and clear his mind. Kevin paced around his ball, trying to get all the factors in focus. He took his stance and stared to the green, but the trap beckoned to him like a gaping monster. His hands trembled. He backed away.

He retook his stance. It was now or never; he must put his ball on the green. He resolved himself to fate, brought his club back and swung. He caught the ball cleanly, arcing it high towards the flag, but then it started to lose momentum and fall. It hit the fringe of the green, bounced back, and sank straight down into the trap. Kevin's heart sank with it.

Ron was waiting anxiously behind the green for Kevin's sand trap attempt. Now he saw he had the game cinched. He sensed the victory.

Kevin agonized over his difficult lie in the sand. It looked like he was dead, literally. He began pacing back and forth from his trapped ball to the pin, trying to get a feel for the shot. The hole was a good 80 feet from his buried ball—all downhill, a wicked rise in the middle.

"It'll fly out of there for sure," George commented.

"Shut up!" Kevin snapped, glaring at him.

George fumbled in his pocket for the reassuring presence of the gun. He might need it if Kevin blew this shot.

Kevin stood hunkered over his golf ball, digging his feet into the sand, trying to get a firm footing. He stared up at the sky as if asking for divine intervention, but there would be no salvation from above. Kevin must now execute this impossible attempt to sink the ball in the hole.

Kevin lowered his head and once again committed himself to fate. He brought the wedge down with all his might. Sand exploded up onto the green, and the ball appeared, streaking across the turf. It sped through the rise, picking up speed, charging the flag. Ron watched in horror as the ball hit the pin, popped straight up, then plopped back down into the cup. A birdie three!

Kevin whooped like a madman. He raced out of the trap, screaming, "Yes! Yes!"

Any bystander watching this little drama would have guessed Kevin had just won the Masters. But of course, this shot was much more significant than that.

Now it was Ron's turn. The putt he needed for victory was now for a tie on the hole. This putt was for life or death.

Ron steadied his nerves, trying to conceal his shock. His head was reeling—the green spinning around him as if he was in some surreal nightmare. Ron took his stance and measured the shot, but the cup seemed to pull farther away. The putter felt heavy as lead. He couldn't shake off his nerves; it was no use. When Ron tapped the ball, it trickled wide of the hole.

He had lost.

There was no one in sight in any direction as George came forward with the gun. "Shall we go, Mr. Jakes?" he said, pointing towards the woods.

As they entered the copse, Ron thought of making a run for it. He would be a moving target for the small Derringer. But why risk it? When Kevin gets the gun, surely this farce would be over.

"Kneel right there!" George ordered when they reached the clearing.

As Ron bent to his knees, George suddenly snapped a pair of handcuffs on his wrists. Now his arms were helpless; he had no escape.

"Congratulations, Mr. Brown," George announced to Kevin as he handed him the Derringer. "It seems you're a wealthy man. Now all you have to do is complete the agreement."

Kevin took the weapon and walked over to Ron, who was helplessly trying to get back to his feet.

"Throw it away, Kevin," Ron pleaded. "Let's get out of here."

Kevin said nothing.

"What the hell are you doing?" Ron yelled. "Throw it away!"

Kevin pointed the gun at Ron's head. His face cold as ice.

"For God's sake, Kevin," Ron screamed. "I wouldn't shoot you!" Kevin hesitated, then he lowered the gun back down.

George stepped forward. "Don't listen to him, Kevin. Do you think if he had won, he would come back here and throw the gun away? Take the money!"

Kevin raised the gun again. "He's right, if I hadn't made that sand shot, I'd be here on my knees Ron, you'd have the gun, and I'd be good as dead."

By now, Ron was a quivering mass, pleading with Kevin. But it was no use.

"I'm sorry, Ron," he said, his voice cold as ice. "It's two million dollars!" He pointed the gun, turned his head away, and pulled the trigger.

A sharp BANG echoed through the woods.

There was no immediate slumping of the body. Ron remained kneeling. His mouth was agape, his face a death mask. Kevin turned his head back.

There was no blood?

Suddenly, the clearing filled with George's laughter. "It's BLANK!" George roared. "It's phony! As phony as this watch, and this check."

Kevin stared dumbfounded at George. "What! What's going on?"

"You bought it all, you greedy scumbags!" George roared again, trying to contain himself. "Even I didn't believe you two were so greedy—that you would go this far."

Ron struggled with the cuffs. He screamed at Kevin in a fiery rage. "You tried to kill me, you son-of-a-bitch! Get these handcuffs off me!"

Kevin backed away; he was emotionally spent. He slumped to the ground.

George pointed to the cowering Kevin. "Look, Ron, there's your partner. Is he shocked because he thought he'd killed you, or because there is no money? And you," he turned to Ron, "you couldn't wait to get back here when you'd thought you had won. To you, Kevin was already dead meat."

George reached into his pocket, pulled out the handcuff keys, and threw them on the ground.

"Have fun, guys," George said. He then began walking away.

By now, Ron had somehow staggered to his feet despite still wearing the cuffs.

"You owe us money, you bastard!" he screamed after George, spit flying from his mouth.

"So, sue me," George yelled back. He took the recording from his pocket and held it up. "This will make for some entertaining evidence in court."

"Wait!" Kevin called after him. "Why did you do this? Why us?"

George stopped and turned on the trail. "Do you remember an elderly man you scammed here two years ago on this day?"

Kevin shrugged.

"I didn't expect you would," George replied with disgust. "You snakes played him beautifully, didn't you? You pretended to be his friend, acted like you were duffers just like he was. Then you took him for everything he had, right here on the sixteenth hole. He left the course a broken man. When he got home, he collapsed with a stroke. I know. I watched him die. He was my father."

"So?" Ron yelled after George as he walked away. "He knew what he was doing. He wanted to play."

George looked back at Ron with all the contempt he could find. "Yes, just like you two scumbags did today."

The big rented Bentley pulled out of the parking lot and drove down the road leading away from the clubhouse. As the car reached the gate, the guard smiled and waved the driver through.

"Have a good round today, sir?" the man asked George as he drove by.

"It was beautiful. Thank you," George replied. "Most rewarding round I've ever played."

A COMMAND PERFORMANCE

A light rain was beginning to fall. Umbrellas came out as shopkeepers scurried to move their wares back undercover. The low evening sun bounced off the streaking drops, making them shimmer like golden harp strings sending an eerie glow over the streets—unusual for the city.

For Dudley, it was an annoyance. He didn't like distractions in his daily walk home. Now he would be late for the old Dick Van Dyke reruns, and that would throw his muffin and tea time off.

Dudley usually had his umbrella with him, but it was broken, and there was no place nearby to fix it, except for O'Malley's. Rylie O'Malley was always waving his hands around, talking so loudly you could hear him from the street. People like O'Malley made Dudley nervous. Why should he answer their prying questions, engage in their needless chatter? All he asked for was a simple service.

No, Dudley would not go into O'Malley's. Instead, he would walk eight blocks to 33rd Street, where no one knew him. That's where he'd search to have his umbrella fixed.

For twenty-two years, Dudley had trudged this same route for work—a solitary drab figure, gray as the pavement he trod, held tight by the bindings of the invisible clock that guided him; obedient to every crosswalk light and painted line; always clutching that same old baggy briefcase. No one ever noticed Dudley. He was an unremarkable face in the crowd. If asked, his fellow workers had little to say about him; he was shy, quiet, kept to himself.

Now we might pause here with some alarm, because that's how neighbors might describe a psychopath after he had shot 22 people dead at a Walmart. But not Dudley. He never displayed any aggressiveness or racism, or even mild anger. He was a meek, timid soul.

Soon the rain was falling heavily. Dudley retreated under the canopy of a nearby shop, as the storm raged against the pavement. Dudley moved further back under the canopy.

Something strange happened this day, something different from all the thousands of days Dudley had trudged these streets. But it wasn't the storm; it was something else. How many times had he walked by this pawnshop, never once noticed its existence? Now he was stranded in front of it, held captive by the storm.

That's when he noticed the ship captain's hat in the window. What was it about this old hat that intrigued him? Was it the light glinting off its shiny brass emblem? He had never been out to sea, or anywhere else for that matter. But somehow, someway, it summoned him. Whatever it was, it wasn't the rain but fate that pulled him into that shop on this day. Dudley hurried inside and made his way over to where the hat was perched. Soon the shopkeeper appeared from somewhere among the musty, nose-biting decay of the artifacts that filled the shop.

"Help you?" he asked.

"I'm interested in the captain's hat," Dudley replied.

"Hat? I don't know about any... Oh! Yes. THAT hat! They don't make quality like this anymore," the man declared, pounding the dust off it as he retrieved it from the window. "I got it from an old sea dog; he was from somewhere in Calcutta, so he was."

The shopkeeper paused to give a far-off look. "He told me it once belonged to the captain of a mighty four-master. Sailed round the Horn, he did. Feel the quality of it, sir," he said, handing it over to Dudley.

Dudley ran his hand along the edge of its brim. Even in its timeworn state, his reflection appeared in the deep, black sheen of its visor. He brought the cap to his head; it slid on easily, almost sensually. It not only fit his head, it embraced it. From somewhere deep in his core, Dudley felt a euphoric rush of power, the likes of which he had never known. He let his fingers fall smartly to his side from its golden braid—like an officer returning a salute.

"How much?" Dudley asked.

"Well, I don't know—a valuable piece of Americana, it is. I hate to part with it. How 'bout 200 dollars cash?"

Dudley didn't haggle over the price, he bought the hat outright.

That night Dudley placed the hat on a chair near his bed. Somehow he was drawn to it. It was speaking to him, telling him of exotic places he had never seen, adventures he'd never known. Dudley lay awake for hours, thinking of the sea and great ships. He wondered what ancient stories the hat could tell him, the secrets it could share. Then, finally, Dudley drifted off into an uneasy sleep.

Soon watery sea-green dreams washed over him in giant swells of ocean foam. He found himself standing upon a pitching deck, his hands grasped firmly to the wheel. A salty sea mist nipped at his face, as the blue horizon rose to meet him. He stood at the helm of mighty tall ship, her rigging full to the wind. He was master and commander of all he surveyed.

Then he fell into a deep slumber and did not stir until daybreak.

The morning's crisp air greeted Dudley as he left his apartment. He checked his seaman's chronometer watch. Damn! He was running late. He quickly shifted the leather case containing his navigation charts to his other hand. There would be no time to walk this morning. It would be better to catch a taxi.

"The USS Draconian driver," Dudley roared as he threw his case into the back seat of the cab. "And make it fast!"

The driver looked back at Dudley, perplexed. "Don't you mean the Draconian Fidelity Life Tower?"

Dudley had no time to mince words. "I said FAST, man!"

The driver quickly jerked the car into drive, and they shot off down the street.

As they drove, Dudley eyed the dark menacing clouds in the eastern sky. He didn't like the look of it; he would have to take the Draconian out early, while the sea was still calm and not a threat to a harbor-bound vessel.

It was beginning to rain when the cab pulled up to the front of the tall gray skyscraper. Dudley left the car and entered the building. His footsteps echoing loudly off the marble floor of the Draconian Tower's lobby.

The desk guard glanced up warily at the apparition wearing a sea captain's hat quickly approaching him.

"Dudley?" the puzzled guard asked as the man drew nearer. Dudley ignored this breach of formality from a low-ranking seaman.

"Send all boarding crew to their stations immediately!" Dudley announced to the startled guard. Then he disappeared into the elevator.

The door to Anne Armbrewstor's office swung open with a bang, startling her. She wasn't used to this kind of intrusion. To her astonishment, Dudley stormed into her office and plopped his briefcase down on her desk.

"I'll be on the bridge," Dudley barked at her. "Kindly send Master Wainfield there at once. Also," he added, "see to it that all other staff officers are summoned here as well."

Anne stared at Dudley in shock. "What, what do you...?"

Dudley ignored her. He walked into the boardroom and shut the door behind him. Seated around a large wooden table were several people chatting and sipping their morning coffee.

"Ah, good, you're already here," Dudley announced as he circled the table. "Don't bother to get up." He went over to the window and stood with his back to them, studying the darkening horizon.

Arnold J. Wainfield reached for his cell phone as his big, sleek limo entered the parkade of the Draconian Tower. He punched in Anne Armbrewstor's number.

Anne came on the line, but she sounded peculiar. "Everyone's here for the board meeting, Mr. Wainfield," she told him. "But I'm afraid there's a problem."

"Problem?" Wainfield didn't need any problems, especially in a board of directors meeting. "What do you mean, a problem?"

"Well, sir, it seems someone has taken over the meeting."

"Who?"

"Dudley, sir."

"Who in the hell is Dudley?"

"I believe he's from central files, sir," Anne nervously answered.

"Well, get him out of there."

"I've tried, sir, but he's very forceful. So I..."

Wainfield interrupted her. "Get his supervisor up there NOW! Dammit!"

Anne winced as he clicked off his cell.

A steady rain began to rinse against the boardroom glass. Dudley shook his head and turned, facing the group at the table.

"Do you see those storm clouds, officers?" he announced, pointing to the window. "We must leave port at once!"

The stunned group sat silenced as Dudley began pacing around the table, staring at the back of each person as he passed. Suddenly he stopped directly behind one of the members.

"Do we have full steam in the boilers, sir?"

"Boilers?" the man weakly replied.

"The boilers, man, are they fired? Do we have steam?"

"Well, I don't know, I..."

"Well, why don't you, mister?"

Dudley quickly turned to the man beside him. "And you, sir!" The man promptly sat bolt upright in his chair. "Have you notified the harbor pilot?"

Before the startled man could answer, Dudley turned to a woman to his left.

"You, Ensign. Have you alerted the crew to stand by?"

No one dared speak to the commanding presence hovering over them. Dudley strode to the head of the table.

"It is my opinion," he announced, "that this vessel is UNFIT to SAIL!" He turned his back and went once again to the window.

Arnold Wainfield came storming off the elevator. Anne Armbrewstor was waiting nervously to meet him. With her was Al Wilcox, Dudley's supervisor.

"This Dudley character work for you, Wilcox?" Wainfield barked at the man.

Wilcox was visibly shaken; it was the only chance he'd ever had to meet the boss, and it was for some weird screw-up from one of his clerks.

"I can't understand it, sir," Al began. "Dudley is a model employee. He's just a mild-mannered recorder, sir."

Al grimaced. He couldn't believe he'd just made an embarrassing reference to Clark Kent.

The boardroom door flew open and in came Wainfield, with Al and Anne trailing behind him. Wainfield spotted Dudley by the window. He gestured to Al to go forward.

Al made his way around the big table and approached the man. "I think you better come with me, Dudley," Al said, touching his arm carefully.

Dudley said nothing. He still faced the window.

"Please, now," Al pleaded.

Wainfield was growing impatient. He quickly paced over to the window. "Mister," he yelled, "you better get back to your section now, or you're going to find yourself unemployed!"

Suddenly, Dudley turned and met Wainfield head-on. "STAND DOWN, SIR!" He roared in the man's face.

The words blew into Wainfield like a broadside of cannon fire, stunning him into silence. He stood frozen in his tracks, dumbfounded.

"Stand at attention when you address your captain, sir!" Dudley boomed again.

Winfield's Italian leather shoes snapped together with a loud pop. He stood arrow straight as his Commander circled him. Dudley didn't like dressing down a senior officer in front of his crew like this, but the situation called for strong measures.

"When your captain's ashore, mister," he began, "it's the responsibility of the First Officer to ensure the ship's readiness. You've been derelict in your duties, haven't you, sir?"

Wainfield nodded meekly.

"I can't HEAR you, mister!" Dudley shouted.

"AYE, SIR!" Wainfield obediently yelled out.

"Ensign Armbrewstor!" Dudley snapped, looking over at Anne. "Please escort this officer to his quarters. He's been relieved of his command."

Dudley then turned his back on Wainfield as Anne solemnly led the reprimanded officer away.

The room was now quiet as a tomb, the only sound the rain beating against the glass. Every eye was transfixed on the imposing figure at the window. Finally, after an agonizing silence, Dudley spoke.

"Mr. Wilcox," came Dudley's commanding voice.

Al's face was ashen. He'd already seen his career pass before his eyes. He tried to speak, but his voice cracked into falsetto. Finally, he managed to croak, "Aye, sir."

"Take the helm, Mr. Wilcox."

Al's eyes searched the room desperately. "The what, sir?"

Dudley nodded to the podium near the window. "The helm, Mr. Wilcox."

Al stepped to the podium and grasped an invisible wheel.

Dudley pointed to the man nearest him. "You, sir!"

"Me?" the man gulped.

"Call the engine room, tell them to make way—hurry, man!"

Dudley's voice was still firm but now less strict. "All of you, take your stations," he announced to the startled group. "Aweigh all lines; we're putting out to sea!"

Somewhere deep in the bowels of the Draconian building, a custodian picked up the ringing maintenance phone.

"Furnace room," the man mumbled, gnawing on a doughnut.

"This is the bridge," came the reply. "Bring the ships boilers to full steam. We're casting off."

"We're what?"

"Full steam, man. Now!" the voice ordered, then hung up.

The crew took their positions as Dudley prepared to take them out of the harbor. He barked out his orders, receiving a crisp "Aye, aye, sir" with his every command.

"Steady the helm, Mr. Wilcox!" Dudley ordered.

"Aye, sir, I'm bringing her about," Al answered, amazed at his newfound salty vocabulary.

There was no doubt in the mind of every person there. The mighty Draconian Tower was about to wrench free of its foundation, glide down Main Street, and drift majestically out to sea.

Suddenly, the rooms big doors swung open—Wainfield was back. Once he was out of Dudley's presence, he had found new courage—plus three security guards and two police officers.

"That's him!" Wainfield shouted, pointing to Dudley. "Be careful. He's dangerous!"

One of the policemen approached Dudley, eyeing him warily. "Alright, buddy, we don't want any trouble. You come along quietly now."

Dudley sized up the situation quickly. He had no authority over these civilians. He would have to go ashore and straighten this out. One of the policemen attempted to grab him by the arm.

"Unhand me, sir!" he sternly warned the man. "I'm the captain of this vessel, and you will show me due respect. As we leave, you will walk two paces behind me."

At the door, Dudley turned to Wainfield. "I will deal with your mutinous treachery later, mister." Then he dramatically exited, the two policemen following obediently behind him.

Not far from the Draconian Tower sat the local pub, which was dark and mostly deserted now at such a late hour. Near the end of the bar, lit partially from the soft glow of an overhead TV, sat Al Wilcox. He was quietly nursing a double scotch. He hadn't lost his job, but he would certainly have to lie low for a while.

As he looked up to order another drink, his eye caught the flickering image on the TV screen above him and he gasped out loud. There on the evening news was Dudley, standing next to the Mayor.

"TURN IT UP!" Al shouted to the bartender as he strained to hear the voice of an off-camera reporter.

"Aren't you worried, sir?" the reporter was asking the Mayor. "You will be heavily criticized for this sudden appointment that your council just passed."

"Well, it is unprecedented," answered the Mayor.

"But appointing a new Chief of Police with virtually no law enforcement background of any kind?"

"We were concerned with that, of course," the Mayor replied. "But when we recognized Chief Dudley's remarkable leadership abilities, the way he took over the police station, well, we knew he was our man."

"But Mayor," another reporter crowded in, "we already had an experienced Police Chief. So what does he say about all this?"

"That is no problem," the Mayor assured him. "Chief Dudley has promised us our old Chief will have an important role to fulfill as Assistant Chief under his leadership."

The video cut to Dudley. "Can you give some indication, sir," probed the reporter, "how you plan to manage our city police department?"

Dudley took the mike from the reporter and looked confidently into the camera. "I will rely heavily on the assertive skills I possess in commanding people," he stated.

"I like him," the bartender commented, eyeing the screen.

"He looks like a real leader to me. He'd make a great president."

Al gulped down his drink and ordered another one. He had to admit it—Dudley appeared resplendent in his magnificent new police uniform and police chief's hat.

Or was it a sea captain's hat?

THE BOY IN THE ATTIC

Tommy sadly stood in the yard as his mom readied herself to leave. Then she came over and put her hand on the young boy's shoulder.

"Okay, you have all the things you will need in your case," she told him. "Here's your cell phone should you want to call. But don't worry, I'll be back as soon as I settle things in Portland. We'll have a place of our own again soon, I promise."

His mother then gave Tommy a tight hug, kissed him goodbye, and then got into her car.

Tommy stood with his Aunt Mattie and waved goodbye until the car returned to the main highway in the distance.

"Well, Tommy," Mattie said, "let me show you to your room."

The boy had mixed emotions about staying in Aunt Mattie's country house. He loved the thought of walking the local fields and exploring the woodlands, but he didn't like the old Victorian house itself. It was interesting to him, but it also appeared dark and foreboding—full of spider webs, creepy.

Elderly Aunt Mattie's farm had no livestock; it was just a single home with a few outbuildings on acreage. She lived there alone with her cat, Gulliver. The place was too far away from other houses with local kids of Tommy's age for playing. Now, with his mom leaving him here, he would only have his computer, a few books, and 90-year-old Aunt Mattie to talk to.

Tommy's mom was a divorcee. She had just lost her last job, and now she was struggling to make ends meet. So she must leave her twelve-year-old son Tommy with a relative until she got things back to normal. That's why Tommy now found himself on this little farm outside Portland, Oregon, on this long, hot summer.

Mattie took out a key and unlocked the door to the stairs leading to the second floor. Tommy thought that a bit odd, but he didn't question her.

"I lock the door when I'm here by myself," Mattie told him. "But don't worry, I'll keep it open for you. There's a large open bedroom at the top of the stairs." She went on, "I'm getting too old to climb those steps now, so my bedroom is down here on the first floor."

Tommy picked up his small travel case. "It's okay. I can take this up myself."

"Thanks, dear. You'll find it's more private up there for you, nice and roomy." Mattie then handed him some keys. "This extra set will get you in and out of the house. If you need anything else, don't be afraid to ask. I'll get lunch ready now. You must be hungry."

The open area on the second floor was a sort of sitting room with a large, frilly canopy bed. Tommy placed his PC on an antique desk and found a plug-in. There was a closet nearby, but Tommy set his suitcase on the sofa. It seemed more convenient. He felt odd in this environment—a lost boy in an ancient storybook manor. He longed for the simple little room he had at the last apartment.

When Tommy returned to the main floor, Mattie had lunch ready on the back porch, overlooking the property's green fields. "Everything okay?" she asked.

"Yes, Ma'am, but I sorta feel a little silly in that huge bed," he told her.

"Well, it is a bit outdated." She smiled back.

"Did that used to be your bedroom, Aunt Mattie?"

"Yes, my husband, Edward, and I had the bedroom upstairs after we bought this place many years ago. So it's just me here now. Ed died in 1989, and I've lived here alone ever since."

"Do you have any kids?" Tommy asked.

"No, sadly, we never could have them. You're the first youngster to stay here for a very long time."

"Who lived here before you?"

"We bought it from some people called the Daytons. They were the original owners, with a large family of ten children."

"Wow! When was that?"

"That family built this house in 1896 and raised their children here," Mattie reflected. "They lived here until we bought it from them in 1967."

"That's a long time," Tommy's young mind reasoned. "So much has happened here, I guess."

"Oh, yes, Tommy," Mattie replied with a broad smile, but there was also a hint of sadness in her eyes. "There is much history here."

After lunch, Tommy decided to explore the rest of the upstairs part of the house. There were a few other rooms—pantries, small closets—but as he tried the door of each room, he found them all locked.

Tommy returned to the main room and sat on his bed. That's when he noticed a door directly across from him. He got up and went to try the handle. This door opened, revealing a steep, narrow stairway leading upward—a definite invitation for any kid to explore. Tommy grabbed the railing and climbed his way to the loft above.

At the top, it opened up into a musty, unlit attic. Dormer windows provided some shafts of light, allowing Tommy's eyes to adjust to the room's dark forms. He could make out old wooden boxes, antique travel trunks, and discarded broken furniture, all covered with dust and cobwebs. It looked interesting, so he ventured in, clambering through the jumble of unused old things. But soon the sun's heat on the roof and the choking dust became stifling. He decided to go back through the mess to leave. That's when his foot hit something, causing a loud clunk. He reached down and picked up a metal device covered with crinkled, worn black leather. The object appeared to be some kind of harness. He put it back and left the attic.

Tommy spent the rest of that afternoon putting his things away and playing a few games on his computer. But the metal item in the loft still intrigued him. What was that thing?

That evening at supper, Tommy ventured a question concerning the strange object he had found. "Aunt Mattie," he began, "I took a peek up in your attic, um, up the stairs."

Mattie frowned, a bit surprised. "Was the door unlocked?"

"Yes, it opened."

"Oh, yes, I forgot that latch was broken. I don't go up there much these days." Mattie's voice turned serious. "But listen, don't you ever go up there again, okay? It's not safe. That old floor above the ceiling is weak."

"Okay, I won't, but I wanted to ask you something. I found this strange metal harness-looking thing up there, covered with leather. What was that for?"

Mattie was a bit unnerved. "You found that?" She paused, then regrouped her thoughts. "Oh, that thing. It's a body brace for a young child who lived here many years ago."

"What's a body brace?"

"It's an old medical support device. One child in the

Dayton family was a boy who had a condition called severe cerebral palsy."

"Is that what the brace is for?"

"Yes, Tommy. It's for a horrible disease that sometimes affects the muscles so much that the victim has no control. So the poor boy had to wear that steel frame fitted to his body so he could walk."

"What was his name?"

"It was Rudy. He died when he was about your age. Now listen, we should not dwell on such things. That was long ago. You finish those potatoes. I've baked a strawberry rhubarb pie just for you."

Tommy's face lit up. "Wow, I'd like that! I think. What's rhubarb?"

"It's a reddish fruit stalk that's quite bitter. But don't worry, the strawberries make it just the right degree of sweetness. You'll like it."

Mattie opened the oven door of her old cast iron stove, and the sweet aroma of the pie filled the room. "How about that? Smells good, doesn't it?"

Tommy ate two slices of the pie, and Mattie smiled as she watched him gobble it down. The pie was a hit.

Later that evening, back in his room, Tommy read some of his comic books and tried a few more games on his computer. But soon, he grew tired; it was getting late, and it had been a long day coming out from Portland to the country. He was feeling sleepy, yet these strange surroundings were disquieting.

Over the previous year, so much had changed in Tommy's young life. First, his dad had left after a nasty divorce, which was very upsetting. Then, after his mother had lost her job as a store clerk, she had needed to leave him with other family members. He never knew how long he would ever be at anyone's address.

Soon a knock came on the entrance door to the stairs. "It's me, Tommy," Mattie announced. "Everything alright up there for you? Are you ready for bed yet?"

"Yes, I'm just going to bed now."

"Good," she replied. "Now, you put on your pajamas as your mother wants. And listen, if you need anything, you come down here and knock on my bedroom door. Okay?"

"Okay, Aunt Mattie. I will. Goodnight."

"Goodnight, son."

The boy put on his pajamas and turned off the overhead light. But he left the table lamp on; he hated sleeping in the dark. Then he climbed into the massive bed, pulled up the heavy quilt, and stared up at the ceiling. He was uneasy; everything was so uncertain. However, Aunt Mattie's kindness to him was reassuring, helping him settle in and deal with things. But even so, one more new surrounding had only left him feeling more wayward and lost.

A noise came. A scratching sound. Tommy jolted up in the bed, but then he heard a soft meow. It was only Gulliver, Aunt Mattie's cat. She called him 'her traveling cat'.

Tommy arose from the big bed, tiptoed down to the first-floor stairs door, and opened it. Gulliver rushed in and went straight up to the bedroom. Tommy climbed back into bed with him, holding the big furry kitty close; its purring was reassuring, soothing. All was better now. He tried to close his eyes again.

But still there was that dreaded door at the foot of his bed, leading up to the attic. Rudy's brace was up there—almost a hundred years it had lain there. Would Rudy come back for it?

Tommy turned over and stared at the door handle, watching it. That door was unlocked—would its lever turn at any moment? Might something come down from that dark attic and open this door? He fixed his eyes on the handle, waiting for it to move. Chills began to run up the spine of his young body. He tried to remove these thoughts from his mind. He held Gulliver tight and closed his eyes. But every creak, every groan from this spooky old house popped his eyes open again, causing him to look once more upon the handle. The night grew darker outside and the wind rustled through tree limbs that brushed against the roof. Moans and creaks emanated from old loose boards and left-open shutters. Sleep finally came, but it was a fitful, restless sleep.

There is no measure of time one can use when awakened from slumber. There is only disorder and confusion—is this real, or a dream, blurred by imagined reality? Suddenly Tommy became aware that he was hearing an actual sound, but it was the wrong kind of noise—a scraping and scratching on the floor above him.

Oh, God, let it be a bird on the roof! He jerked tight the covers and locked his eyes once again on the lever. He fixated on it—eyes wide open, frozen to that door. Then, another noise came, the sound of the handle moving—turning, making a creaking, latch-clicking sound. SOMETHING was opening this door!

Gulliver sprang from the bed and flew from the room.

The door groaned wide open, revealing a dark shadow that filled the doorframe. It lurched forward in a human shape! Tommy jolted upright in bed, fear paralyzing his body, his throat so tight he could not scream. The specter approached, walking bent over, its body braced in a metal, leather-covered cage, its feet scraping on the wooden floor. It stopped directly in front of the bed. A ghastly aura surrounded its torso and a tortured boy's face appeared. Then the vision raised an extended arm and spoke.

"Will you play with me?"

Tommy shrieked, a scream that pierced the night; his face locked in terror. He leaped from the bed and rushed for the stairs on a dead run. He lost his footing and tumbled headlong down the steps, crashing into the heavy door at the bottom. The boy jumped back up, grabbed the door handle—it didn't budge. He pounded on the door, yelling for Mattie. He looked back up the stairs. Was the phantom coming? His heart was drumming so fast; he barely could breathe.

He heard Mattie's frantic voice from outside the door. "Tommy, turn the handle!" she yelled.

"The door won't open, Mattie. It's locked!"

"It's locked from the inside, Tommy. I can't open it out here!"

The terrified boy realized he must go back for the key. If the phantom was coming for him, he was trapped down here. His only choice was back up those stairs.

"I'm going now!" he yelled to Mattie.

There was no carpet on the risers; Tommy's footsteps on the oak boards made a thump, thump sound, even though he was tiptoeing on the wood. Then, finally, he reached the top step and peeked in. The big room was empty—no sign of Rudy.

Tommy looked for the keys, but he couldn't remember where he had put them. Then he saw his cell phone on the table. He went to the phone, grabbed it up, and hit his mother's number.

She answered, "Tommy?"

"Mom, it's me! Come quickly, I'm…."

A voice suddenly cut in, "Tommy!" It was Rudy's voice, a mournful, far off eerie sound. "Why won't you talk to me?"

The boy threw the phone down in terror, ran over to the bed, dropped to the floor, and rolled under it.

Something was tickling Tommy's face. He looked up to

find a trembling Gulliver. The cat had found him on the floor. Tommy listened for a sound, watched for Rudy's feet rattling along the floor from beneath the bed, but he saw nothing. He waited, listening for Rudy, but didn't hear him. He rolled back out, and tiptoed to the window.

Outside he could see a figure on the lawn. It was Aunt Mattie, walking around the house. Tommy pounded on the glass, yelling, "Here, Here!" But she disappeared from view.

Tommy turned back to the room, frantically checking his pants pocket for the keys—but no! There standing by the sofa was a human figure—it was Rudy!

Fear swelled back in Tommy's throat. His first urge was to scream again, but he held his breath, settled his nerves, and turned to face the apparition. The figure seemed less threatening now, even friendly.

"Hello, Rudy," Tommy said.

"Please don't run from me," Rudy begged. "I just want to talk to you."

"I will talk to you; I, I can be your friend."

Rudy struggled to come closer; his body was bent awkwardly by the metal brace, forcing his trapped torso into a rigid stance. His limbs were twisted strangely like a broken robot toy, the metal foot brace scraping on the floor. Clunk—scratch—clunk!

"Don't laugh at me," he pleaded. "The others all laughed, made fun of how I walked. Will you be my friend?"

"I won't laugh, Rudy. I'll be your friend." Tommy's voice was jittery, but he tried hard to be convincing. "Why have you picked me?"

"You're the first boy to..." Rudy stopped to collect his words. "Since the others left me here alone—I had no one to talk to since THEM!"

The sudden emphasis on 'them', startled Tommy. "You say

they laughed at you; why didn't your mom and dad make them stop?"

"Nobody stopped them—too many children here." His voice now took on anger. "I was a freak to them. They made fun of my walking, jeered at me. I had no one to tell how I felt; how I ached in my heart for a kind word, a gentle, caring touch. But NO! All of them laughed!" He raised his fist, shaking in rage. "They laughed at my pain, my suffering!"

Tommy sensed that talking to Rudy seemed to make things worse instead of helping, but he still hoped to find some connection. "I'm listening to you, I hear your hurt, and I want to be your friend."

"No. No! You ran from me. You hate me too!" Rudy swung his arm around, knocking the lamp from the table. "You're just like the others!" he yelled.

"No, Rudy, I don't hate you!" Tommy could see the broken lamp was sparking. A small fire was starting. "I was just scared, that's all."

"You despised me!" Rudy raged back. "Look at me. I'm a monster! I must wear this cage of metal forever. Why couldn't they see me, not it?" Rudy struggled down the hallway, his brace creaking and groaning. "I wanted them to stop. They all must pay for what they did!"

Tommy rushed to the lamp, but the dry carpet beneath it was now flaming uncontrollably. He tried to beat the fire out, but it was too late. It had begun spreading up the curtain behind the bed.

There was no escape now. Tommy was trapped on the upper floor of a burning house. He ran around the room, looking for some way out, as the flames raged up the walls. His only chance was the big front window. He started for it, but a sudden flash of fire erupted on the drapes, pushing him back, the heat searing his arms. He ran to the only other window.

He spotted Mattie frantically waving below. She was shouting for him to unlock the catch on the sill. Tommy looked to the side and saw the lever; he grabbed it and yanked it back. The old frame wouldn't budge. He kicked it with his foot, and it snapped open. He scrambled out onto the porch roof.

"Slide down the drainpipe," Mattie yelled.

The way down was a long drop, but the pipe held as Tommy slid down to the ground.

Mattie rushed over and embraced him. "Thank God, you're okay!" she cried.

Tommy was sobbing uncontrollably. "Aunt Mattie, Rudy was there. He's in the house!"

He's gone now, Tommy. You're safe, and nothing can hurt you anymore."

"I did'nt want Rudy to leave, I didn't hate him, he thinks I hate him."

"I believe he knows that Tommy. He's gone to someplace better now I'm sure."

Soon the raging fire of the old house could be seen for miles across the valley, a flaming beacon of a bygone past now bowing out. Fire trucks were there, but it was a lost cause. The old structure was burning to the ground.

Tommy and Mattie stood far back from the heat of the building, staring at the blazing Victorian as it gasped its last breath.

"Your mom called me, Tommy," she informed him. "I told her you were okay. She's on her way."

"Did you know Rudy was always there, Aunt Mattie? Did you ever see him?"

"No, I never actually saw him, but I sensed his presence. Doors would be unlocked and relocked. But I'm forgetful; so I thought maybe it was just me. I would hear strange noises and put them off. That's how I dealt with it."

Tommy looked up at Mattie, his voice as earnest as he could make it. "I saw Rudy, Aunt Mattie. I heard his voice. I talked to him!"

"I believe you, Tommy. But, think about this: if what you say about Rudy is true, then he didn't want to hurt you. He was a boy, just like you. You awakened his spirit when you came here, but at the same time, a hatred caused by his abuse locked inside him was rekindled. A hatred so strong it lasted, even beyond death."

At that very moment, the last remaining wall of the house collapsed into the smoldering ashes. "I'm sorry you lost your house, Aunt Mattie," Tommy said. "All your things are gone now."

"That's no matter—Thank God you got out of there alive. I have insurance. The place had old wiring."

Just then, a meow sounded, and Gulliver appeared. His fur was singed, and smoky, but he was okay.

"Oh my God!" Mattie exclaimed. "You made it out, you stupid, silly kitty." She picked him up, and held him. "He's one traveling cat for sure."

"Aunt Mattie," Tommy added, "I just remembered something. If they check the cell phone call I made to my mom, Rudy's voice will be on it."

Mattie laughed. "If it is, Tommy, it'll be on every news talk show in the country."

That night on the evening news: Feature story just released. A startling discovery on a cell phone call reveals a voice thought to be that of a ghost in a burning house. Get all the details tonight on CNN's Don Lemon live…

THE MESSAGE

HELLO SAD LADY!   WHY ARE YOU SAD?   GOOD NIGHT, SAD LADY.

Raymond leaned slowly back in his chair and gazed out the window. He wasn't looking for anything in particular, just needing time to think. He exhaled a long slow breath, causing his shoulders to sag and his chin to drop; making him look far older than his fifty years. The room was quiet except for the soft tick, tick of the antique brass clock he kept on his credenza. Finally, he shifted his gaze from the window to the tall, slender woman standing before his desk.

"My God, that's it? That's all there is?"

"That's it," Jane said. "Trust me; we've scanned every log."

Raymond turned the paper over and over in his hands as if it might speak to him and reveal its strange secrets. Then he laid it back on the table. "It's a childish mystery—how can we release this?"

Jane saw the same look of frustration on Raymond's face that she had felt when she first read the message. "We can't keep it under wraps for long, Ray; the entire facility knew it came in."

Raymond folded the note and handed it back to her. "Is this the only copy?"

"Yes. This, and of course, the printouts down at Arecibo."

"When did it come in?"

"Approximately 0227 Puerto Rico's time."Raymond now

knew why Jane looked so tired. As his chief project scientist, Dr. Jane Tanner would be the first person in Houston to be informed when this message arrived.

"My God, Jane, if we put this out cold without some explanation, the implications would be devastating. The crazies will be out of the woodwork. There's no telling what can happen!"

"I hear you," Jane replied. "But what the hell does it mean? It's beyond anything we expected. After all these years of listening, waiting, we get this riddle."

Raymond shook his head. "We've got to stall as long as possible."

Jane put the note back in her pocket. "I'll get back to Arecibo right now."

Before she could leave, Raymond turned from the window. "Have they pinpointed where it came from?"

Jane hesitated, parsing her next words carefully. "From Negus 5, the 4C41.17 sector."

Raymond's face turned ghostly pale. "Oh, my God!" he gasped. "Isn't that…?"

"Yes," Jane interjected. "It's on the edge of the known universe, fifteen billion light-years away!"

Jane punched in the code for Arecibo on the satellite link at her desk, and Dr. Emil Hoffman came on the line. "Emil," Jane began, "I hope you're not as baffled down there as we all are up here?"

Emil's voice was unusually excited. "Jane, we don't know whether to laugh or cry. This message has really thrown us for a loop."

"Emil, listen, we've got to keep a lid on this until we can all meet and get a chance to analyze it."

"We could have a problem," he replied. "There's a bunch of Caltech students down here, and they'll know something big is up for sure."

Jane winced. Now the rumors would be flying. "How many people have seen the message?"

"Everybody on shift, but we've kept it limited to just them."

"Good," Jane came back. "I'll be down with a team as fast as I can."

Before she could congratulate Emil on the discovery, he accidentally tripped the disconnect, cutting her off. Jane smiled to herself. The ordinarily staid astrophysicist was definitely not himself.

The flashing light on Raymond's private line told him that his secretary wanted him. "Yes, Alice," he answered.

"Mr. Willington, there's a reporter from UPI on the line, and she's very persistent."

"Good lord!" Raymond gasped. "They've sniffed this out already? Okay, Alice, put her on."

"Mr. Willington, this is Ann Morris," came the voice on the phone. "We have an unsubstantiated report that you've received an alien message transmission at your Arecibo radio telescope. Can you confirm or deny this?"

Raymond paused for a second, searching for the right words. "I cannot comment at this time," he answered. "However, this office will release a formal statement at the very first opportunity."

After he hung up, Raymond looked at the vast star map that graced his wall. It's beginning, he now realized. His disciplined world of science was about to be turned upside down.

The air suddenly became cooler as the crowded van left the coastal plain and began the long, winding drive up to the Arecibo observatory. Lush tropical forests closed in the roadway on both sides, shielding any view of the wide Puerto Rican mountain range beyond. The enormous telescope that stood ahead was not what most people think of when they think of a telescope, but a massive 305 meter wide dish placed in a valley between several mountain peaks. The Arecibo radio telescope was the most significant listening device on the planet. It was part of NASA's HRMS project, the High-Resolution Microwave Survey, scanning the universe looking for signs of extraterrestrial life.

As they bounced along the dusty mountain roadway, Jane reflected on the many late hours she had spent sitting at the approaching scope's control panel, monitoring data pouring in from the night sky. Now, the smell of the damp, misty air brought back a flood of memories, reminding her how much she missed this place and the people she had left here.

Finally, late in the afternoon, the dusty van, with its weary group of scientists, arrived at the site. They parked by a scattering of makeshift buildings that sat near the edge of the gaping dish.

"Jane!" roared the big burly scientist. Emil dropped the readouts he was studying and gave her a bear hug. Suddenly, a loud cheer reverberated through the control room. Soon everyone was gathered around, showering her with welcoming applause. Emil produced a large bottle of champagne.

"Surely you didn't believe we'd drink this without you, did you?" Emil had kept the bottle in his desk for 33 years; now, he broke the seal and poured. He put his arm around Jane and held up his glass. "Here's to Dr. Jane Tanner. From day one, she fought hard for this project, and now more than anyone, she deserves its success."

As they cheered, Jane suddenly became embarrassed. Emil had surprised her with this unexpected attention, and now she was at a loss for words. "Dr. Hoffman," she began, her voice becoming emotional as she held up her glass, "bought this bottle the year we broke ground in 1973. Many scoffed at our goal here. But all of you kept the faith—especially you, Emil. And now I want to tell you this is the best-tasting champagne I've ever had."

As Jane began to drink, the events of the last 24 hours suddenly came crashing down on her. She had been in boardrooms too long and away from science. Here was what it was all about. Here they had just made scientific history. Tears welled up in her eyes. She looked at Emil; he was crying even harder than she was.

The noisy children playing in the sand sounded just fine to Honrich Linden. As the busy chief scientist for Bell Labs, his vacations were few and far between. As he sat on the warm Hawaiian beach, galaxies and far-off worlds were the last things on his mind. Suddenly the soft music on the patio's small radio was rudely interrupted!

"Reports released minutes ago from a top official source at NASA have been confirmed. Scientists at their huge radio antennae in the Caribbean have just received an alien radio transmission. The message itself has not been revealed. We repeat, a high..."

Honrich jumped up and grabbed his beach bag. "Honey, get the kids. I'm sorry, but I'm afraid our vacation is over!"

Even though Jane had only had 24 hours to assemble a team for Arecibo, the group of scientists gathered in the briefing room bore impressive credentials. Included were Dr. Neville Bronski, who, along with his associates, had won the Nobel Prize for their work on the origins of the universe; two of Cornell's top astrophysicists and theorists on Quantum Mechanics; plus many others from Cambridge and Yale, who had come as quickly as they could for this historic gathering. And now they all sat like nervous school children as Emil scratched out the message on the blackboard before them.

When the word "HELLO" was revealed, a loud cheer and applause broke out among the group. But then, as Emil slowly chalked in the rest of the message, the room grew disturbingly silent. Jane scanned the assembled faces. It was almost a replay of Raymond's reaction when she had showed him the note back in Houston.

Finally, Emil broke the ice. "I would now like to introduce you to Dr. Alan Thomas."

Up before the group came a blue-jeaned kid with a bright red shock of unkempt hair and freckled boyish features. Jane wondered if this young scientist was aware of the coming celebrity that would soon catapult him into the world's spotlight.

"Alan is a radio astronomer visiting us from Berkeley," Emil informed them. "He is the person who unlocked the code."

Before Alan could begin to speak, he was peppered with a cacophony of questions from around the room.

"Order! Order, please!" Jane broke in to gain control. "One at a time, please!"

When all had settled down, Dr. Lee Ito from Columbia University stood up. "Dr. Thomas, are you sure this wording is real, and not some phenomenon of scrambled signals, that by coincidence you mistook for code?"

Alan was calm and measured in his reply. He unrolled before them a long printout with yellow markings identifying many different sections of signals. "This is just the English language section here," he began, showing one area to Ito first, and then to the other gathered scientists. "Since the exact time it came in, we have identified a match to over 8,000 world languages!"

A stunned silence came over the room.

"See this section, Dr. Ito," Alan went on, pointing to an

underlined section of the printout. "It's in the ancient Bantu dialect. There are 13 languages in the Bantu grouping alone, 681 sub-languages in Bantoid and 1,514 in Niger-Congo." Alan looked to the other scientists, who were by now clearly visibly shaken. "In fact, this code not only arrived in every written language known, but in sub-dialects we have not spoken in over 1000 years." The young scientist held up the printout and exclaimed to the astonished assembly, "This message contains a coded written history of world languages that goes back to the very beginnings of recorded civilization."

The room burst into loud clamor again, and Jane once again had to call it to order.

"Do we have a consensus here, everyone?" Jane boldly asked the group. "Is this an authentic message from extraterrestrial intelligence?"

Suddenly Dr. Bronski arose. "This is all very interesting," he announced. "But I want an answer to the million dollar question before I vote, and that is, EXACTLY where did this message come from?"

Jane held her breath as Alan went over to the star chart and pointed to Negus 5.

"This is PREPOSTEROUS!" Bronski angrily shouted. "I cannot accept this. It's a trick, a fraud! I will not be a part of this delusion." The great man stormed from the room.

Soon, others solemnly stood up and followed him. Alan was left standing alone, silently holding his printout. Jane felt the urge to say something, but instinct told her it would be useless. The world of science would now divide into many camps. There was no turning back. Those that stayed here this day would be her allies in the fierce battle that lay ahead.

Rain poured relentlessly against the bronze glass sides of the NASA research building just outside of Houston.

166

Everything in Texas is extreme, including the weather. When it's hot, Texans can fry eggs on the hoods of cars. When it rains, it comes like a splash from a giant, overfilled bathtub. It hits the ground so hard that it bounces back up, drenching everything and rendering umbrellas useless.

In the meeting room next to Raymond's office, Honrich Linden briefed Raymond and fellow HRMS scientist Lou Jarvis on his announcement strategy for the press. Honrich had hastily worked it out during his urgent plane trip back from his ruined vacation in Hawaii.

"We must keep the scientific agenda in a study mode," Honrich began. "We cannot infer anything about the message's purpose. Nothing other than: we are working on it."

Raymond had listened carefully to Honrich's plan. "What about the religious connotations, let alone the junking of modern theory?" he reminded him. "This is a vital moment, Honrich; we are about to release a message that proves we are not alone in the universe. Think of that!"

"Ray, we can't hold back any information," Honrich added intently. "By this time next week, much of it will be out—whether we announce it officially or not."

Ray got up and stood at the window, looking out across the rain-soaked complex. "We must be proactive," he asserted. "The message must be guided, explained somehow." He turned and looked at each man as he spoke. "We need more experts involved. There must be some explanation we can use? Hell! I'm ready to go to the pope if need be. I realize we are just the messengers here, gentlemen. Still, we have a responsibility to see that this doesn't produce a world crisis."

Ray's comments voiced the apparent concerns that all three men had agonized over. No one spoke. The only sound came from the rain beating on the window.

"Well don't everyone speak at once!" Ray finally added.

Nervous laughter filled the small room.

Soon Lou Jarvis spoke up. Lou was also an astrophysicist like Honrich. "We can't possibly reorganize the last 100 hundred years of scientific theory in two days," Lou began. "But we can at least assemble enough of our colleagues to try to frame a model."

"No!" Honrich quickly came in. "Everyone is split on this. You heard about Bronski walking out of the Arecibo meeting. Without his endorsement and those of the others, it's not credible."

Ray turned from the window. "Then, who? Academics? Teachers? Theologians? New Age theorists?"

"There is one man," Lou replied.

"There is such a man?" Ray asked.

"Yes. And I never thought I would say this. Nathan Whitesides."

"Oh, my God!" Honrich groaned. "Not that crackpot."

Lou paused to form his words carefully. "He's the most brilliant mind of our generation. You know that, Honrich; he was once your mentor."

Ray looked over to Honrich. "Is this true?"

Honrich placed his pencil down and pushed aside his notes. "Nathan Whitesides is indeed a great mind, and he could have been the finest physicist of our generation. But he branched off into mysticism and mumbo jumbo theories of the universe. Even the radicals think he's a fruit bar."

"Yes, he's an eccentric," Lou admitted. "But he was one of the first to say the universe is speeding up in its expansion when everyone else was saying it was slowing down."

"I'm against it, Lou," Honrich shot back, getting agitated. "Damn it! We'll be the laughing stock of the world of science. Is that what this has come to?"

Raymond reached into his papers and took out the

Arecibo message with the words TOP SECRET stamped on it. He passed it over to his chief officer. "Honrich, have you forgotten what this message means?"

Honrich said nothing.

The two other men in the room could see the frustration on Honrich's face. He knew more than anyone the implications of the message's impact. Traditional science was now totally upended, and radical belief would soon become the order of the day.

"I know him," Honrich finally replied with resignation. "He won't receive anyone. He's a bloody recluse."

"That's right," Lou agreed. "We have scorned him too many times. He hates us all. But he might see you, Ray. I've never mentioned this, but he's a big supporter of HRMS, and he would respect you as its main founder."

"But I'm not a physicist," Ray replied, feeling insecure. "I'm just an astronomer, and for the last 20 years, I've been a damn desk jockey. He'd eat me alive. One of you will have to come with me."

"No, Ray!" Honrich answered, his voice as sincere as he could make it. "You should go alone; Lou and I are obsolete now. As the leader of the Search for the Extra-Terrestrial Intelligence Project, you are probably the only man he would see."

"Alright then," Ray sighed. "Let's get him on the phone."

Across from the campus at Cambridge University sits the sprawling brownstone resident professor's housing area. Here, world-renowned scientists discuss complex mathematical theories as they travel along the worn brick walkways to classes at the main campus.

As Raymond entered this area, he carefully studied the little brass nameplates adorning the doors that were tucked into the ivy-draped brick facades.

The alien message Raymond was carrying in his pocket made him edgy as hell. There had been reports that radical groups would kill to have it in their possession. The Academy had insisted on a police escort, but Whiteside's directions were explicit: "Come alone, or don't come at all." Nevertheless, a bevy of security police, and military snipers huddled out of sight behind the tall oaks bordering the campus parking lot.

Finally, Raymond came to the doorway of Nathaniel Alexander Whitesides, Ph.D. He carefully knocked upon the heavy wooden door. Soon, a small, dowdy woman in a simple print dress came and opened the door, then quietly escorted Raymond down the inner hall until she arrived at a doorway. She stopped and gestured for him to enter, then she disappeared from where she had come.

The room was dark at first, the only light coming from a skylight above. A strong aroma of old musty paper and dust instantly attacked his nostrils. Tall bookshelves, stacked with hundreds of tomes, reached to the ceiling. Raymond made his way around high piles of even more books that had found no place on the crowded shelves. He rounded the corner, and there, at last, was revealed the great man himself.

Whitesides sat perched behind a large wooden desk. A pipe stuck in his mouth. Smoke trailed its way up until it was indistinguishable against the yellow stained ceiling. The man was intent on some manuscript before him and only acknowledged his guest by pointing to an overstuffed chair. Raymond settled uncomfortably into the chair and sank until he was looking up at Whitesides between his knees.

Whitesides extended his arm towards Raymond without looking up from his reading. At first, Raymond thought he was offering a handshake, and then he remembered the message. Ray dug down into his pocket and produced the paper. The professor took only a second to read the note, and then he laid it on the desk. He leaned back in his chair and stared in deep concentration out the window.

Five minutes passed by as the two men sat in silence.

Raymond felt highly uneasy. He glanced at the many book covers to occupy his mind during this maddening quiet. He was surprised to observe very few scientific journals. Instead, there were many titles on Zoroastrianism, Zen, Taoism, Kabbalism, and other obscure religions and mystical beliefs he had never even heard of.

At last, Whitesides spoke. "Well, Mr. Willington," he announced, "a fascinating little message. What do you think of it?" He stamped out his pipe and leaned back in his chair.

"I am more concerned to know what you think of it," Raymond replied.

"Me? What can I possibly add to it, sir?"

Raymond sensed Whitesides was playing a little cat-and-mouse game. He decided to play along. "Well, for one thing, they say you have insight into matters where others have often failed."

"They say? Who are they?"

"Does it matter?" Raymond replied.

Whitesides looked at him sternly and said nothing. Suddenly, he produced a small bottle of cognac from a drawer and set it down on the desktop with a bang. A wry smile crept onto his face. "Of course, it doesn't matter," he answered. "Care for a drink, sir? I find it helpful in clearing the cobwebs sometimes."

The sudden friendliness caught Raymond off guard. He sensed he had passed some little test, and now it would be a great insult not to accept his host's offering. "Yes, I would. Thank you," he told the man.

Whitesides arose and bellowed out down the hallway. "ILSA! Bring our guest a glass. Quickly now!"

Soon Ilsa was there, and Whitesides poured the cognac.

"Well!" Whitesides exclaimed, "I had hoped that someday the universe would speak to us, and here you are, Mr. Willington." He tipped his glass in a salute to his startled guest.

Raymond joined Whitesides in a bit of toast. Then he got to the matter at hand. "What do you think it means?"

"Ah. You are looking for an answer?" Whitesides asked.

"Yes, something. Anything."

"There can be no answer," he stated flatly.

"I don't follow," Raymond responded incredulously. "This message implies that intelligent life predates our universe, that someone knew about us before we even existed. It was sent over 15 billion light-years ago in every language we have!"

"No! It was sent only yesterday," Whitesides replied.

Raymond tried to gather his composure. "I can tell you, sir, that it came from the deepest part of space."

"Of course it did. Actually, much more than 15 billion light-years away."

Raymond set down his glass. Now they were getting into multi-dimensional theory. "Are you saying it came from another dimension?"

"Many would say that," Whitesides replied. "It helps to ease their little minds." He held up the bottle again. "Care for another drink?"

"I'm gonna need one," Raymond answered, trying to get his head around the enormity of this last statement. "Are you saying String Theory is for simple minds?"

"That theory is already passe, now the flavor of the month is dark matter," Whitesides stated with a dismissive gesture. "It's much bigger than implied dimensions; it means that we can't measure time-existence in our terms." Whitesides filled Raymond's glass again. "May I call you by your first name?"

"Yes, of course."

"Ray," he began, "there can be no answers because we have

no questions, its beyond our science,"

"But the message itself asks a question," Raymond noted. "It's sent to us, but it seems to be referring to someone else. Who is this "Sad Lady"? Why is she important?"

Whitesides produced a broad smile. "Ah, yes. Charming, isn't it? But why does its meaning have to have reason? Can't we look at it as our friendly little note from space? That is its true importance. Our technology can no more reply to it, than this pipe in this tray can tell me to stop lighting it. You looked for a message Ray, and you finally got one."

Raymond wondered at Whiteside's reasoning. "Then why was it sent?"

"I told you—we cannot answer."

Ray gathered his thoughts. "I'm a scientist, sir. My religious beliefs are irrelevant, but this message will shake religion to its foundation. Many will doubt the existence of God!"

"Oh, but God certainly does exist," Whitesides replied, somewhat amused. "And you're looking at him."

"What are you implying now?"

"I'm saying we are all God! God is in us. That's really what many ancient writings have said all along."

Raymond was growing tired of this game. "Religion sees God as the creator."

"Yes, and that's what we are," Whitesides replied.

"And what worlds have we created?"

"Why our children, and their children, and beyond. Without our minds to perceive existence, these worlds don't exist."

"But God is eternal."

"We are all made of the eternal atomic chemistry of life. You and I, and the distant beings that sent this message. If you are looking for God, Ray, look inside yourself."

Raymond's frustration was getting the better of him. "Sir, over half of this worlds population believes in a separate all powerful god, I cannot turn them off by attacking their faith."

"Thats how God works, sir, you can leave it at that."

"I'm looking for logic here, Nathan, and all you are giving me is riddles."

Whitesides picked the Arecibo message up and handed it back to his guest. "You are the one who came bearing riddles!" He snapped back at Raymond. "Now you talk of logic!"

Raymond slumped back down in his chair. Damn that message, he swore to himself. It defied all reasoning; it was like a slap in the face. He took his cognac up and sipped its contents, rolling the sharp liquid around in his mouth.

Whitesides offered him the bottle again. "It does help, doesn't it, Ray? Another drink?" His voice now softer. Raymond nodded, and Whitesides refilled his glass. The cognac was loosening Raymond up a bit now.

"Is it that straightforward, Nathan?" Raymond began, looking for some common ground with his newfound drinking partner. "The staggering complexity of the universe?"

Whitesides gestured to all the books in his library. "Look at all this knowledge, Ray. I have struggled my entire life to put it into mathematical equations. I looked for answers in a formula. But as I reached each roadblock of understanding, I realized that the truth lies beyond the nuts and bolts of science. If I had the infinite power to pursue it all, I would not find a final solution, but an endless chain of transition. Eternity is so elegant, Ray, it forced me to seek other explanations, beyond our known sciences."

"But what of us," Raymond challenged, "isn't that the ultimate truth? Now that we know we are not alone. What do we tell the world?"

"Questions, questions, … Ray, have another drink."

Raymond could feel the cognac work its smooth liquid magic. He relaxed and let the deep, enfolding chair hold him like a womb. He considered the startling events of the last two days. He thought of his team members, Honrich and Lou, now forced to doubt a lifetime of study. And the rebellion at Arecibo; now he wondered if it all was that earth-shaking and necessary.

"I'm trying to understand you, Nathan, but I cannot grasp that there is no answer in science. What are you expressing here?"

"The great truth of existence." The professor's voice was now becoming almost passionate. He set down his glass and leaned forward. "It means that our minds are the true power in the universe, Ray—not gravity or Black holes or subatomic particles—but the pure essence of human thought. That's when I realized what the ancients meant; the ability to achieve connection through a receptive mind."

"But sir, our brains waves travel by electrical transmitted neurons, they're limited to that."

"Yes, but that is the way the body's brain waves travel—something we can measure. Para psychological transmission is way beyond that."

"Are you saying our minds, our thoughts, enter somehow into the realm of another dimension where they travel beyond the speed of light, a form of thought transference?"

"Well how about that Raymond? You've finally grasped the ultimate universe!"

"I have grasped nothing, sir. You're talking about spirituality."

"No Ray! It is an actuality! Its essence is not encumbered by the boundaries of our science. We can ponder thought beyond the physical world, and cross the cosmos in seconds. It's life's most rare gift, and your radio telescope has received it."

"I'm trying to understand you, Nathan, but how can that possibly be explained?"

"That's because you have jumbled your mind with our world. The Arecibo message speaks to us of only one thing. Expect everything—life owes us no explanation. All has been tried, until we understand each new miracle after endless trial. One of those miracles is our very existence here on this tiny asteroid. When you accept that, Ray, then you are free from all boundaries, and nothing will mystify you."

As Raymond finally prepared to leave, he turned to the scientist once more at the doorway. "Nathan, I cannot accept your mysticism as the answer, but I am forced to accept the fact that the message is real. Is there anything I can tell everyone, anything that will help me with this arduous task?"

Whiteside grabbed Raymond's arm and held it firmly to show conviction in what he was about to say.

"Tell them the message gives our lives meaning within this vast universe. Life, death, and rebirth are our eternal cycle, but there also will be discovery, correction, and reasoning. We must get past our small world and out to the stars and know our place among them. That's the one thing that you can tell them, Ray."

Then Whiteside released his hold on the man, turned back into his house and shut the door.

Lisa carefully removed the doll from the painted toy box under her bed. She took the doll up and examined the locket around its neck. "Why does she have a locket, Mommy?"

"Your granddad put it there so it would never be lost," her mother replied.

"What's inside the locket?"

"Open it and look, Lisa."

Lisa snapped open the small case. Inside on the lid was an engraved inscription.

"Why don't you read it?" her mother asked.

Lisa silently read the tiny poem. *Milk and silk and ice white moons. Rust and dust and stars on spoons.*

"What does it mean?"

"Granddad engraved it there. He told me there's an entire world inside it, and those are some of its things."

"How did he know about the world?"

"Granddad worked at a place called a space observatory. One day he discovered this far-off place, but no matter how much he tried he couldn't talk to them. So the lab decided they were just too far away, and gave him other work to do. But Granddad couldn't just throw away his discovery, so he put their secret location in this locket and gave it to me when I was a little girl. Then when you were born, I gave it to you."

"What's the doll's name?"

"I called her Sad Lady because she looks so gloomy."

"Can I try to talk to the world in the locket?" Lisa asked.

"Well, granddad and I never thought of that," her mother laughed. "Who knows? Maybe they'll hear you!"

Lisa opened a second small lid and revealed a glistening Crystal, she put the small locket close to her mouth.

"Hello Sad, Lady!"

Lisa waited for a reply, but none came from the doll's little painted face.

"Why are you so sad?" She asked the doll.

"I believe Granddad picked her because he couldn't talk to the world," Her mother answered. "So he was sad too."

Lisa's mother looked up at the clock on the bedroom wall. "It's time to put her away now. It's way past your bedtime."

"Goodnight, Sad Lady," Lisa said, she closed the little locket and placed the doll back in the painted box with the other toys, and pushed it back under her bed.

Brad Bennett lives with his wife, Norrie, in Oliver BC, Canada's wine capital in the heart of the Okanagan Valley. Since retiring as a graphic designer and art director, Brad and Norrie have enjoyed the pastoral beauty and friendly existence the area offers. Norrie enjoys touring the vineyards and shopping the local farm markets. When Brad is not playing pool, or visiting his grand children with Norrie, he is avidly pursuing his lifelong dream of writing short stories, fiction, and non-fiction. He has published two books, and won two international short story contests.

Acknowledgment:
*Special thanks to **Kathryn Graham** for her expert story critiquing and proofing guidance to keep the written text true and accurate.*